RUNNING

into

TIME

A JOURNEY BEYOND

DOUGLAS R. BLACK

ISBN: 978-0-9863-9790-5 (sc)
ISBN: 978-0-9863-9791-2 (e)

Library of Congress Control Number: 2015903129

Lulu Publishing Services rev. date: 6/9/2015

Here we sit in silence
into dissonance we ride
here we whisper violence
in each other's minds we will confide
facing what may come, with a stand against reality
knowing at least we are on the right side.

Here do we fashion our makeshift dreams
nursing our lives' wounds,
should we come apart at the seams
it's renegade living, harsh and unforgiving
through golden memories and silent screams.

Here do we tell tales of victory and defeat,
here we look back on ecstasy, despair, and deceit.
It's an uneasy condition, alongside concrete tradition
a blessing in disguise, exposed only through the right eyes,
life's expedition, a guide to the skies,
some written record of times we felt so alive.

For JML

1

In times of old we practiced this art.
for meaning, exaltation, or transport to the skies.
Though our vessels cling tight to the earth,
through this careful proficiency do our flailing hearts rebirth.
And my story, in full, will one day be told, if only to a few isolated ears
of how the Runners and their kin spent their daze, weeks, and fears.

"Let's move." A young boy's voice slid across the floor of a small building in a faint whisper. The structure accommodated a line of four turnstiles, with two metal cages on either side housing blacked-out windows. The place was devoid of any activity, save the steady pulse of a dim, repeating light emitting from a ticket machine that looked as if it had been on the business end of a baseball bat.

A young girl appeared from behind a corner in the vestibule, just short of the small set of stairs leading down to the ticket area. She was slim and athletic, not tall by any account, and of agile frame and posture. Her ashen-blonde hair was drawn about the sides of her pale-white complexion, set back into a long fountain ponytail. Her eyes were concealed behind dark sunglasses that served only to prevent a meeting of gazes with some curious stranger, for it was long after dusk, and not a trace of the sun was left in the sky. Juli was garbed in her usual style, extravagant and carefree, vivid colors throughout.

She was accompanied by another adolescent of similar stature, his own disheveled appearance – in ripped jeans and a black hoodie fastened about his waist – conceived simply out of disregard for any form of prejudgment. He wore a black skullcap, the lower seam giving way to a curtain of unkempt brown hair that hid his eyes.

The sunglass bit was out of the question for Atris anyway. He claimed it was almost insulting to the sun, to shield the eyes from something that sustains all life. What an evolutionary blunder: the danger associated with ultraviolet radiation. He figured driving was the only obvious excuse for shades, though truthfully, he'd never driven during the light of day. It was only under the trustworthy cover of darkness that he and his companion could navigate the asphalt veins of suburbia undetected by the rampant swine. Otherwise, they would be instantly branded mischievous deviants, their youthful faces betraying them as soon as they passed the first cop looking up from his game of solitaire. Plus, mother needed the car during the day.

"The way the wind flies," Juli whispered. She leapt forward from Atris's right and down the stairs, peering around the far corner beyond the turnstiles. She smiled back at him before bracing her hands on two of the stanchions and gracefully bounding over the metal spindle. Atris watched his friend disappear up the long staircase to the right and followed her example without second thought. A train whistle sounded in the distance.

A few minutes later, the pair was facing down-rail on the last car, floating by sporadic labyrinths forged of streetlights.

"Do you think we'll find it tonight?" Juli asked, breaking the hypnotic drone of the tracks below.

Atris didn't look up from the pages resting on his lap. He only lifted his pen from the paper for a moment's response. "Well, all the potential is there."

"Yeah," Juli sighed, not breaking her stare out the rear window. "Tonight's accounts?"

Atris closed his pen and sheathed it in a small nylon holster affixed to his belt. He found safekeeping for his ink more crucial than the sheath's intended use of housing a small flashlight, even though soon they would be navigating darkened streets. They didn't need any light source; they had greater methods to utilize in their search, means far more intangible.

"Well," he started, clearing his throat. "Twelve October, o-five. Act one, already within. Tonight's mission!" His voice was projected and concise. "We will cancel the restart, find Juli's ledger, and reconfigure our hearts." Atris grew eager, indicative in his diction's decline. "To race past the part of physical walls we've defined through years of realistic resignation and a lost sense of art, while the world goes blind."

Juli laughed shyly. "Good." Atris placed the notebook on her lap as she produced her own polished silver pen, capped with a red jewel. She dictated as she wrote, with Atris listening intently and taking in the view.

"Act two, if only we knew." She governed ink in gorgeous swirls, the words flowing seamlessly from her mind and through her fingertips. "He and I, travelers forever, architects of the life force. No one ever knows what's in store. Draw the curtain, lock the door. For together we'll shape a world inside these walls, born of sheer energy and the promise in truth to each other." The train banked into a sharp turn that sent Juli against Atris. Her concentration and pen falls were unaffected.

"The uncommitted need no fear of recover, 'cause we've tended these scales for a lifetime now, and none on this level operate with higher precision. We have found the means to a secular eternity. One projected from within, drawn out through the din, from the depths of the mind, off the surface of the skin."

The land about them disappeared, opening the skies ahead. The light emitting from their destination smothered the stars. A pronounced rhythmic procession sounded beneath them as the train made its way across the bridge. Juli tossed the book to Atris and sprang to her feet. She looked out the window and down the dark river below, its shores littered with all variations of lights beating back the blackness. This was the way they liked the world. The city was open. It was a late Wednesday, yielding few herds of drunks and partygoers wandering the streets. There were only those working the graveyard shift, restless hobos, and a few isolated others not the least bit concerned with two young wanderers.

Juli let the mood darken as the city grew closer. "I sure am glad we have these opportunities, Atris."

"How do you figure?" He rose up to join her by the window.

"A whole society, driving itself mad. We live in an amazing world, but most people move too fast to appreciate it. They're tied up chasing some fleeting notion of security they may never find. I wonder how much time we have left until we have to do it ourselves, to work to live and live to work."

"It doesn't have to be so bleak," Atris responded. "It's true, everyone is after the quick fix. Most believe the simple key to happiness is having more money. But I'm sure we'll find our own way, far from this crowded state. We just have to believe and never lose sight of that goal. Plus, that's a long way off. There's no need to worry now."

Juli smiled again. "I guess you're right. It really is irrelevant. Like you said, just have to believe. And hopefully we'll find each other when we come out the other side." Atris nodded and reached out to hold her hand. Juli figured the one regulation that would get her through anything was to believe in herself, no matter what. Atris shared the same general viewpoint, though he attained the end result via different avenues.

It was indicative in how the two came together, in day and night fashion, in the turbulent serpentine trials of adolescent self-discovery. There weren't any guide books or advice from an older friend or sibling they could take for a shred of its intended worth. It was a process they had to evaluate themselves, among those they held closest – the very same ranks that would more often than not prove just as clueless.

Laying down the foundations for individualism was handled in many ways. They figured lashing out for position to be the most efficient and rewarding, bracing against life as it came to carve their own route, defining right and wrong through risk, despair, trial, and triumph. They would hold on through the testaments of time, through the very best and crushing worst of days, and see who had the rigid faith to never surrender to the gray.

Juli had come to believe life was best faced single-handedly: never attached, never hurt. Contrastingly, Atris promoted forefront precedence of the well-being of friends and brothers; self-validation was sure to follow. This was the only critical outlook they didn't agree on – by a large margin.

Juli would say careful scrutiny was needed when sticking by one's friends. One had to evaluate those around them with the most open of minds as well as the strongest of lenses. In truth, she often walked a fine line between arrogance and apathy. She saw Atris's compassion as an obstacle that dragged him down and rendered weights of those who simply wouldn't make the same levels of sacrifice as he.

Atris collected himself. "Wind's howling pretty good out there."

"It is," she agreed. "We'll fly then."

The train departed the bridge and plummeted below ground. All was dark around them. The distant future was decisively granted minimal attention. To live for the moment was doctrine. The future would be upon them soon enough, and there was no use fretting about it. Concern for it was even ranked among concern of death.

And the past? Well, the past was defined through their collective stories and shining memories. The finesse involved in a wondrous life was keeping momentum. This proved difficult in its own right, in the raising of the bar, with many later adventures falling short of previous victories. They had to remember it wasn't a test; that living in the now simply was striving to live at their best. Nothing can change the past. It's just a gauge to measure by.

Juli and Atris's night was before them, and all rudimentary reservations were made to fade away. It was something fleeting they were after, as if life had come to a peak already and the bell curve of wonder and glory they had drafted into their lives was reaching its terminal point. This seemed certain, and the aversion was palpable.

They were both secretly battling horrific doubt – worried they were getting older too fast, understanding the roads ahead all too well and concerned their lives would conform to the choking city grids above instead of the mountainous switchbacks and open highways they longed for. They suspected things would inevitably begin to take a turn for the structured, the dull and the dragging.

It had long been a rising desire among the lot of their kind to be let loose upon some great struggle – some primal bout in good versus evil, something worth dying for even – to prove that the radiance in life that had been dimming as the years went by was indeed not spent.

"So where are we going?" Juli asked.

"Well, for now we're heading wherever the line is taking us."

The train banked right and gradually slowed, the screeching of brakes bouncing off the tunnel as it came into the station.

"I wonder how much time is left." Juli bit her lip and surveyed the linoleum floor.

Atris figured she was still adrift in deeper tides. "Well, you know me, I'm an avid fan of the mind over matter principal. Though alcohol is always helpful." He produced a small flask from his pocket. "We have the night! Best get moving, 'fore you end up on the west side."

The train came to a halt, and Atris made for the opening doors.

Juli smiled at Atris's enthusiasm. "You'd still come back for me," she stated from the shadows.

Atris revisited their outlooks on the avenues of belief and reliance. He laughed, "Of course I would. Sometimes all we need is a friend to pull us out of the dark." He stepped back over and helped her to her feet.

2

There went another whim, a division, a collision stemming from the storm within.
What was under was torn to fly the tide back to the day we were born.
Though those kids we knew have adapted to the cold, their harbors fortified,
their borders sold to the shadows they were forced to know.
But how did it all go?
There are volumes now that speak in tongues, in dying languages for deafened ears.
A perverse magic hanging now only to whispers as the dream is beaten back over
these exiled years.
Now there's no laughter, no love, no wonder, nor tears.
Just a longing, a waiting, a calling, that hope which was deemed dead still burns in
the stars, watching over us while retracing the scars it left behind.

A tris staggered as he backed up across the black of his bedroom floor. The door was shut, securing him within the temporary safe haven of his home, giving him perhaps a few minutes to catch up with himself and collect his thoughts – which at this point, were orchestrating pandemonium across all his senses.

"Dying to know, just where we'll go now." A voice came from within as his footing faltered and he fell to the floor, still clutching his pen. His ledger had long since been lost to the wilderness. This was but one of the crucial problems at hand, and it grew more pressing with each minute elapsed.

Getting out of this mess would prove increasingly difficult if there was no accounting for how this all happened. It had to be in the book; the answers often were. This practice was a matter of second nature to Atris, necessity even: always have some written record to trace. Then again, they had pretty much broken all the rules already, and new strategies would have to be called into play to overcome the current dilemma. They were too far along in the game to be concerned with protocol already violated.

"All right. Got to regroup, return for the others," he whispered to himself. "That must've been three miles back there. Damn good thing we made it without being spotted."

Atris shook his thoughts aside and felt blindly about his desk, searching for the switch that would enlist light to combat the unfolding paranoia. He tended to get carried away with himself in the envelope of total darkness, when his senses were robbed of reference points and his imagination would redline to compensate for the lack of formidable distractions. Complete silence now coupled with total darkness in a menacing alliance that had the potential to wreak substantial havoc at this accelerated rate, for in the obscurity of true solitude he'd find a certain variant of voyage. Myriad memories flooded his mind, now blasted back into speculation: every place he'd ever ridden, every dashboard that ever lit his face, every girl he'd ever embraced, every chase, every narrow miss, every crushing blow, every green field, every time it ever snowed.

He stopped himself, finally catching his quarry and flinging illumination to the walls of the room. The forest had rendered his clothes damp and racked with thorns. It'd certainly been an exigent sprint, but what was the cause of his flight? Where were the others? And how long did they have until sunrise? He couldn't remember.

"You didn't stick to the plan, and now look at you," a judgmental tone said. "Got to get ready before they come at us again."

Atris changed into drier, more durable attire to blend in with the night. It sounded like the rain had stopped, leaving only the wind to persist in its howling, an angered specter in some run-of-the-mill horror film. A tough pair of jeans and the companionship of a trusty hoodie that had seen him through many a misadventure would suffice. He laced up his same rugged boots of course; one must always have full confidence in their footwear.

Honestly, why did people even bother wearing low-cut loafers or those Chuck Taylor deals? There's no accounting for durability and hardly any shock absorption to speak of, no protection in the practical use demands of the real world. Well, their real world at least. Or how all the in-crowd blokes at school always worried about a scuff or blemish on the day's sneaks. The kind of girls Atris and his friends were interested in weren't the type to take an initial liking to someone based on a fresh-pressed collar or some impeccably bleached shoes. Fashion – what a laugh. It had next to no place in the life of a Runner. Moments like these were precise reasons why. Worrying about mud staining the side of your Jordans when the balance of the universe might be at stake was simply not an option.

"Focus."

In a matter of minutes Atris had managed to work his way into a more conducive mindset: collected, resolute, breeding confidence. He grabbed the pen off the desk and holstered it at his side once more.

"Can't be panicking again," he softly reassured himself. "We've been here many times before." *Times?* He wasn't even sure what day it was. He shook off the thought and steadied himself.

In the quietest way possible, he exited his bedroom window and perched on the roof as if a gargoyle of old, scanning the familiar neighborhood streets beyond. The occasional car mimicked two parallel comets rising and falling down the asphalt current as they passed, traveling a hundred miles an hour until he slowed them down in direct observation. The wind wasn't helping him attain the calm state required to approach matters. It was instead best to utilize it, to ride it out and take it for all it was worth. He had known this gale before: fierce, yet brilliant and inspiring as it led him and the others to many a previous point of wonder. Using it would carry the most wayward of spirits in the right direction to victory. It was both trustworthy and certain.

A loud thud against the ground was followed by a tangled swirl of limbs and cloth as Atris came out of the roll and instantly to his feet. The fence was an easy bound, producing little noise to alarm the neighbors. What time was it anyway? There were no lit windows as far as the eye could see.

It was but a quick dash across a couple well-known roads before he found himself back within the concealing woods, determined to regain his lost scriptures and the company of his brothers. Given the proximity of the homes around the forest entrance, he figured it unsafe to utilize his headlamp just yet. The swine might still be on the prowl, and even in his wavering state he was confident enough to negotiate these paths of his own volition.

The moon hung full in the sky and provided generous light through the minor hindrance of scattered clouds. Atris allowed himself to become lost in the view through the trees for a moment, observing a massive ring of light surrounding the great disc in the sky. He had seen it a few times before, the most recent occurrence – well, the only one he could recall in full – was years ago, back when Greer was still alive.

They'd stood together, necks craned up at the marvel above, the pungent smell of smoke caught stiff on a faint breeze. The wind had been calm, no problems or hardships to speak of, only good conversation between two friends as the rest of the crew slept inside the safe house that Atris's home proved to be that night. He couldn't remember what had transpired between he and Greer, what wild notions and proposed theories came from the void that morning, so many long years ago.

Damn! Spotted! Atris leapt from the path and dove into the ditch below. On a normal night, this would've been foolish in light of the ruckus produced by a full-extension dive into leafy concealment, but the wind was doing a fine job of suffocating most foreign sounds, thereby alleviating some chance of detection. The figure ahead didn't show any indication it had discovered him.

Atris was locked in waiting for the moment, turning over the probability of being sighted in his head. The clouds rolled across the moon once again as the figure made its way toward Atris's fortress of foliage, stopping only a few feet away.

"This wind marks a wild night."

Atris was leveled with a cascade of momentary shock, having heard a voice not his own for the first time in what seemed an era. The wind manipulated the dialogue, preventing any solid identification via its owner's tone.

Whoever was there must be indifferent to his plight; otherwise, he'd be under attack right now, and the common enemy wouldn't travel without searchlights. His reasoning was sound, and Atris emerged from the leaf pile to confront the mysterious silhouette.

"But, you're—" He was in too much disbelief to be afraid.

"Not among your plain anymore. You're right, man." Greer ran his hand across his forehead. "But when was the last time something made sense out here anyway?"

His friend's visage came out of the past. Greer was quite thin, an intelligent, rebellious soul that mirrored Arka at first glance, notably differing in his black hair. They both stood a few inches above Atris's sixty-six.

"Last time?" Atris asked. "What ti—? I mean, dammit, it's good to see you!" Atris's demeanor shifted wildly, replacing prevailing caution with excitement. He forced composure, positive he wouldn't forgive himself should he spend this breakthrough encounter in a state of denial or dread. "Whatever madness is going on this night, there is providence in it yet."

Before Greer could respond, reason beset rationalization and landed Atris on the conclusion that he must be conversing with merely an illusion projected of his own mind. This gave way to fear.

What if he had died himself? And perhaps that was the cause for all the confusion? He considered asking his spectral friend.

"Don't even think that," Greer started. He sighed heavily and looked up at the moon. "But you best find the writings you're looking for. Do you remember how to get there?"

"Get there?" Atris gave Greer a sidelong glance. "To the pits? Of course. The trouble is finding out where Arka, Ewan, and Aislin went."

Greer crossed his arms and moved a few steps closer to him. "You mustn't give up hope."

"Well, if we can − steady." Atris was talking only to himself again, sadly focusing his vision on the once more empty path ahead. His heartbeat slowed, his insides doing the wave was getting old and he stifled his adrenaline flow, rationing it for later. It was important to keep a certain level of reassurance, lest he become easy prey for the insidious scourge patrolling the nearby roads. He allowed disappointment to dissipate and cultivated courage: find the book, find the others, get to the bottom of this.

Onward he pressed. His footsteps seemed to be hitting the ground more heavily than normal, as if the metaphorical weight on his shoulders was passing into physical manifestation. No worry. At least he was progressing at a steady speed, almost halfway to the fire pits and hopefully some clue as to the whereabouts of his comrades. Maybe everyone would still be there, having a good time just like how the night must have started. What had happened?

He stopped running for a moment, fishing for some arbitrary hint to an answer. Closing his eyes, a churning fire slowly came into focus. The vision followed with Aislin's image seated safely on its far side, her radiant orange hair flowing about her shoulders, blending almost seamlessly with the shifting warm hues of the dancing flames. Her amber eyes were studying the pages resting on her knees as she delicately grasped Atris's pen, spinning it around and through her pale fingers. She looked up to send a smile his way, shocking him back to the present.

Why did you leave her there?

He frowned.

"That's not something I would've done." It didn't make sense to him at all, but why couldn't he remember anything else?

"You must have left everyone when the cops closed in, ran off. You know you're the fastest − no!"

Atris closed his eyes again and saw lights cutting through the edge of the forest toward their fire's soft glow. It was as if this simultaneously set off an explosion beneath the seat of his friend Ewan, as he took to his feet and cast Atris a look of terror.

"Bail!" he shouted as he rocketed off for the far side of the clearing, leaving nothing but a burst of dirt and mulch where he had sat. Atris glanced to his left to see Arka was already following suit.

But where had Aislin gone? His pulse began to race again.

"Task at hand," he reminded himself as he returned to his present state of solace. *Wait a minute – where the hell was the phone?*

Everyone had the standard comforts of a cellular communication device these days. It's a good thing he reasoned it'd be a liberating experience to leave it at Arka's house before this whole exploit started, so as not to be bothered by the prodding interferences of the outside world and all the secondary players in his life. Good thing, indeed.

Even more liberating was nailing his wristwatch to the wall in hopes of freeing himself from the grip of deadlines. Ah, the irony. The measure of time reassures the mind of forward progression, regardless of goal or reason. It provides simple certainty that the present wouldn't continue to repeat itself should matters go awry – a horrible notion in this case as well as, sadly, several others before it.

He stopped abruptly. Recalling the phone being at Arka's unfortunately created no bridge regarding the interim events. *Wait.* Had he just circled 'round on himself? There was just no way. He knew these woods to the core, though it has – *shit! Spotted again!* This time a dexterous leap to the cover of a broad oak was deemed the more suitable move. Was it another delusion that occupied the woods off to the right, or was it actually something real? It'd been a while since he'd seen anyone – or anything, for that matter – that wasn't his own creation. *Maybe it's nothing? Nope, wrong.* A persistent disturbance in the underbrush grew in volume until the rustling leaves died down as the threat reached the path ahead.

All right …so this is bad.

He tried to regulate his breathing, to remain calm; maybe it would just pass him by. He knew the voices within were simply a result of the dose, or maybe just the best defense mechanism his mind could come up with during such times of trial. People do that, communicate internally, in a wide range of forms. The most effective way to work toward certain solutions was to document proceedings, as if to simulate a secondary party, drawing a phantom opinion of sorts. Again, Atris was an advocate for such reviews, a form of setting the board, pouring the subconscious onto paper for the mind to recycle. It was like a train system even, with the information being passengers. They could change depending on how they grew and what they got from different stops along the way.

Hardly a time for trains. The voice emerged again.

Atris heard faint footsteps and heavy breathing grow louder as the source undeniably closed in, coming within a few feet of the tree.

Well, it's fight or flight at this point.

How cliché. He silently argued with himself.

Atris dug around his backpack, again appreciative of the wind muffling the clamor produced. He pulled out his headlamp and a corkscrew, brandishing each akimbo and letting the bag fall to the forest floor. The steps moved closer still.

He held the corkscrew tight; it was the best he could come up with.

The disruption was almost upon the tree when the crunching leaves ceased. Every muscle was primed and ready to spring, but Atris allowed a moment to pass before deeming it safe to peer over the trunk's cover to the path. A figure stood silent, looking up to the sky, its back turned toward the mighty oak.

Atris nodded to himself and leapt out, activating his head lamp in an attempt to blind the tracker should it turn around. As it did, the wind stopped. The face was made a mirror. Atris stood in stasis, staring at himself as the internal roller coaster plummeted yet again.

There wasn't a sound to be heard, save the uneasy breathing between the two of the whole. Then came the lights again, cutting through the trees from further down toward the path's origin. Atris's mirror image crossed his arms and sighed.

"Look, we've got to move. There is no time left." The doppelganger extended his arm toward the lights before dashing into the darkening madness of the wood and dissolving into nothing.

Atris blinked in disbelief. "All right, I can explain that. I've been talking to myself all night and that hallucination was just the byproduct of being in a psychoactive panic and not having anyone around to help sort things out." They shouldn't have broken the rules in the first place, but they hadn't intended to do so from the start, had they?

It was now to be a full sprint down the trail. The pits were close, and there was still some time before the lights would gain on him. After that, it was only a matter of continuing eastward, cutting through the forest entirely and into the next town over. They had people there who would harbor him if need be.

The minutes gave way to what seemed an hour until the last fallen tree marking the turnoff was overtaken and the clearing's edge line was in sight. Atris had finally made it to the pits, though the lights had closed the gap some. It wouldn't be long until they were upon him. He broke free of the woods and burst into the clearing. The dim embers of the abandoned bonfire still gave off some heat, struggling to recover from the passing rain. Atris scanned the tree line for any sign of his friends. Nothing.

The Book.

It was under the cover of an overhanging log on the hillside, right where Aislin had been sitting. Atris figured he had about two minutes to find what he needed before he'd be forced to ditch to the next town. Frantically opening the cover, he scoured for any sort of entries from the night that might piece together what happened.

> *A dog is just a backwards god. Or is a just god a backwards dog? The good of the land meets the salt of the earth. Where the power at hand carries the sight we were given at birth.*

That didn't really help, moving along...

> *And the tide continues to rise, against the common sway of our collective love left behind. And you have to stand with me as we destroy this web intertwined.*

Atris hesitated, positioning the book at a different angle to best utilize the intermittent moonlight in his search. Wildly flipping through the pages, he quickly ascertained his efforts weren't getting him any closer to useful answers.

His concentration was shattered as a bright light erupted from behind him. *How had they gotten on his flank? There was no way, unless – it was.*

The break of dawn christened the treetops and cast a pale blue hue over the field, etching out the individual characteristics of trees and hedges on the other side. Uniqueness was granted to his surroundings yet again. Now everything wouldn't be the same general black smear, a stroke of good fortune Atris didn't take for granted.

One more look and then he'd have to run. The lights must still be close.

He turned the page. It was Aislin's handwriting, in the elegant manner of a girl with an inherent love for the arts and a steady hand. He read it carefully as a ray of light pierced through the woods in front of him and hit his forehead.

It's Time to wake up.

Atris rose to his feet and glanced to the sides of the clearing, quickly scouting for another route of escape. There was no more time. He felt the ground give way, and a sensation of being pulled forward took him, as if he was falling into the horizon. An awareness of velocity grew to a point, and he perceived strange waves rippling out of his field of vision. The light grew in radiance, consuming everything around him in a flood of blinding white.

He opened his eyes and focused on a pair of flickering fluorescent tube lights a few feet above where he now lay.

"You're back." Aislin's gentle voice barely overpowered the soft hum they produced as she hovered over him. "I've been waiting for you."

Resurrecting his line of sight was still proving difficult, but Atris slowly made out the delicate curvatures of his friend's face.

"Uh..." His words weren't coming easy. "What time is it?"

Aislin smiled and glanced around to the corners of the white room, bringing her gaze back to his face. "I'm not sure. There's no clock here."

"Where is here?" he asked.

Her face showed a faint hint of worry as her smile faded. "We are within now. And we are running out of time."

The light drained from his vision and all went black once more.

3

I don't recall the purpose, I can't remember its name.
It looks a heavy path ahead us yet
it taunts the noose around our necks,
it seems the sky goes on forever, and in dreams we will surrender
out of sight, out of mind
leisure left aside for room to hide,
care not for the dreamers that were taken by the tide.
It feels right, but we're running out of time.

"No way, man – we can't split up! I'd rather be locked in a basement all night." Ewan was voicing his objection with great fervor and those around him withdrew from the idea for the moment.

"It's not that big a deal, nothing we can't handle. And this stuff is barely working in the first place." Arka moved to dismiss the worries of his distraught friend.

"Oh, sure. Like it wasn't working on Three Ten Five?" Ewan's words enticed a sharp chill up Atris's spine. Everyone there knew the date and its pertinence to the current situation. Its trial and outcome proved the very reason the rules were generated in the first place. It was the ill-fated maiden voyage into forces truly unknown, and it had set the precedence by which most other trips were measured. The journey called for the construction of a worded lighthouse warning of unseen reefs in the psyche.

So it came to pass that, on the 10th of March, 2005, Atris, Arka, Ewan, and Greer were subjected to self-induced severances from reality, along with four subsequent individual nightmares none had been able to describe in full since. Around the following St. Patrick's Day celebration, a council was held and a loose draft of rules was set in place to prevent such disasters from reoccurring ...because of course they had to go back.

They knew once the barrier of what others perceive as real was broken through, once they got a true taste of the other side, there just wasn't any putting that away. Some things change you forever. And the kind of wonder and excitement they'd experienced couldn't be mimicked by any force man had yet produced – at least not any four teenagers from South Jersey were privy to, or could afford for that matter. Four days after St. Pat's, the rules were redrafted to include less fist fights and drinking game rules.

Rule One: Always stick together. Leave no man behind.

Decidedly the paramount concept in Runner dogma, this rule has also become law in many admirable factions throughout history. When traveling to the other side, it's no exaggeration that matters could get as heavy as if you were actually on a dangerous mission. Stick by the guy next to you and you will see each other through whatever hell comes your way. Two, three heads are better than one. An extra pair of eyes is always ...well, right.

Rule Two: Never trip alone.

This rule is broken frequently, its violation justified in terms of amount consumed or the crushing level of boredom at hand; coupled and sealed with the absence of willing company at said time. Though if you are planning on heading to the mental frontier solo from the start, and you think matters don't at least have potential to go awry, you're just a silly person.

Rule Three: Never get stuck. Always have an exit.

Many a time has a venture headed south because parents came into the picture. Sure, it all started out carefree, but when mother comes home from work it's going to be abundantly suspicious to find you and your friends watching lasers dance over the walls. Then you got to factor in the ensuing questions, and why *aren't* you hungry for dinner?

Don't ever find yourself trapped, with fear of having to convince or elude any authority figures. The risk of the snowball factor in this practice is far too high to taunt; an aspect well known amongst the experienced brand. Along with the term "exit" comes an obligation for outdoor access. A little fresh air goes a long way, and the caress of a slight breeze can alleviate a worrisome numbing of touch that may have potential to become frightening. This may deter a severe lulling of senses and acceleration of mind that may shape a spiral impossible to derail from for hours.

And Rule Four: Well, I forget number four; it can be …citrus fruit, for now.

Arka sighed. The first rule was admittedly foremost concern. They were each aware of the terrors that might befall one should they separate from the group, that crushing feeling of abandonment compounding the probability that reality might be ripped out from under them.

"It's just a matter of getting to a safe location. Unless you'd prefer to stick it out in the rain? You have to feel that storm coming." Arka had considered Ewan's angle but was trying to conform to logic, a correlation constantly observed by his kin.

"Well, the deed is done, and things might get heavy, but it's not like we can't find shelter," Atris added. "We've done so before."

Ewan scoffed, unconvinced and persistent. "Yeah, sure. The gazebo or an overpass in the apartments, that's where I want to spend the next few hours."

The sun was going down as the clouds continued to roll in, amassing overhead to mirror the mounting tension among the three wayward explorers. The dwindling light faded from the gray sky.

★★★★

"This is bullshit," Ewan muttered under his breath, crouching behind a bush along the side of the road. There was no telling how long it'd been since he first went into hiding, but whatever drew him to concealment was presumably something that merited an extended stay. He sifted through split images of low-lying branches, entangling thorns, flashes of light, and a flickering flame before he gave up figuring things out in his current fugue. Why couldn't he remember anything? He cautiously glanced both ways down the road and emerged from the woods, heading left toward the neighborhood he knew so well throughout his youth.

"I can't believe we let it happen again." He brushed the pine needles off his shoulders and stuffed his hands into the front pocket of his hoodie. "Play with fire and you'll get – shit. Get that thought outta your head. Just have to find the others." He shuffled down the dark street. "Man, I can't wait to rub this one in their faces. I was right *again* and ignored *again*." It wasn't easy being the youngest of such an experienced trinity. He felt his brothers underestimated his insights due to this fact, despite frequent reassurance it wasn't the case. ... Experienced, right.

The three of them knew life's minutia at this point in the game. They each had hard enough lives, each battled difficulties and formed great triumphs from seemingly nothing. They observed extensive facets of social assimilation, scrutinizing what trending conformity webbed throughout the handful of high schools they pinballed through between the three of them, all the while integrated into a stretching gamut of prospective futures they wanted no part of. No proposed path or profession ever sounded appealing or worth all the worry so many around them were subjecting themselves to.

Sure, further down the line they knew there was a strong possibility they'd be forced to concede to a lesser calling, but their rising awareness of the coming resignation was regarded irrelevant and written off as a waste of energy. The long-term future could wait. It was an ass anyway.

There existed a stark need for adventure; a deep lust for exploration and the unknown. But why? Ewan couldn't remember when he'd lost his natural edge, that sense of excitement attained simply by seeing new places and experiencing new things. His world must have gotten too small, too fast. Some analogy about goldfishes in there. Had it all been another repercussion of adolescence? Was it generated of a bitter stew of stale platitudes, pessimism, and hormones as the brain jockeyed for stability? Was it a biological circuit breaker that the window for conceiving offspring was fast approaching? They say people have children to live vicariously through their amazement with the world as they absorb it anyway. But Ewan knew once someone becomes safe and satisfied with the general scope around them, they face a daunting emptiness. What more could he and his brothers do to chase thrill? How should they go about dealing with this wonder-loss?

Ewan laughed lowly to himself. Maybe his kind were just different, vexed with a predisposition to restlessness. Perhaps it was part of their genetic model even, for better or worse. Other species had predetermined traits and roles to be played throughout their societal structure: workers, caretakers, breeders, soldiers. Perhaps they were destined surveyors, pathfinders, scouts.

And maybe these adventures of theirs were byproducts of all that, like some preset equation trying to balance itself out. Maybe still they were results of too many punk-rock songs promising revolutions that never happened. The search for something greater had to continue elsewhere, and dosing was the best method available at the time. It kept with the ongoing pursuit of perspective and unadulterated freedom. It was by far the most efficient in the breaking free of a cyclic lifestyle, and instant gratification was there to be had.

In their altered world, everything always felt new, even when it sometimes turned out relatively the same. One certainty prevailed: They would never give up, holding out for collective fulfillment for as long as it'd take, despite how winding and treacherous the roads ahead would prove.

And this particular road was wearing on Ewan's feet. His footfalls had been lost on him for quite some time whilst immersed in thoughts of his brethren and why they were the way they were. That was the biggest problem with violating the second rule: He had all the damn time in the world to silently reflect on things. Talking to oneself became common practice in solitary trials, a shameless stratagem for composure when faced with nothing but your imagination, permitted to let fly all shades of the emotional spectrum onto the accepting canvas of the still black night.

Ewan scoffed and flung his arms about, casting off creeping discomfort before pondering matters once more. What exactly was at stake here? What was the best course of action? It had to be after midnight and the streets were no longer safe. He was on edge, primed to leap into the cover of the wood at the first sign of headlights.

This was sadly required of the boys when traversing town in the middle of the night, regardless of sobriety. To chance the lights coming upon their position to not belong to the lawmen could prove a disastrous and expensive mistake. The commonwealths of suburbia thrived off the persistent defiance of their hard-headed youth, eventually rendering most rebels cautious, docile fractions of their former selves. There's only so much one can endure before the court drains them of will and finance. Ewan had to employ the shadows around him and tread carefully between passing lights.

He laughed to himself again; a habit in times of distress that often antagonized those around him – obviously an absent worry in this case. Hell, he could've been so fortunate. His low laughter ceased, and he stopped short in his tracks, glancing into the ditch off the side of the road. Apparently a young fawn hadn't been so adept in dodging headlights. The carefree creature was drained of animation, leaving the cold, gelatinous gaze of empty eyes to peer up at passing travelers. It must've been a strange thing to turn your head and instantly have the life knocked out of you in a single, high-speed blow.

"I wonder if deer have an afterlife." Ewan turned his head in curiosity before abruptly looking over his shoulder. He was forced to dive behind a tree adjacent the carcass as a pair of lights came up on him and flew past seconds later, leaving a wormlike trail of luminescence in their wake.

"This is getting old."

★★★★

Arka was always of a collected manner, more so than the others at least. Being the eldest of the group, his eighteen years granted him immunity from prosecution for simply existing outdoors in the late hours. Thus, he strode confidently, fretting not for detection by any worldly points of authority. He had made it out of the cluttered wood unscathed, readying his last cigarette before crushing the box and stuffing it in his back pocket. His lighter sparked the immediate area repeatedly as if a struggling firecracker that would never see its purpose fulfilled. He compensated for the wind's direction as it subsided. The flame finally started up and danced wildly about his palm.

He thought for a moment on the situation with the phones. It wasn't an optional channel, as he never carried one himself. Of secure standing for now, the only question at hand was where to go next. He figured he must be closest to Katrina's at this point, and her basement had proven sanctuary in previous times of trouble. Perhaps that was where the others would head, if they'd managed to flee in some common general direction.

Arka strolled along the path for a few minutes before the flow of a nearby waterfall gradually prevailed over the whistling breeze. At least he had reached the lake and a good point of reference. Katrina's home was on the far end, further up from the falls, and he designated it his intermediate destination. Arka respected what was going on around him and understood that, while things seemed safe for now, and the shock of what transpired at the pits was behind them, the verdict of the night was still far from certain. Matters could still turn sour at any minute, for whatever reason, and now was no time to remain alone. He left the woodland path and continued upstream along the river's edge.

The flowing water was much appreciated, its gentle babble blending beautifully with the undulating howl of the ominous wind. The woods were oftentimes good as home to the Runners anyway. It was the majority of suburbia that dubbed them the "wrong" place to be, especially at night. As far as the township was concerned, anyone concealing themselves in the wraps of nature after dusk was undoubtedly up to no good, and must be hunted, made example of, and mined in the process. Many an endeavor had been cut short by the need to flee through the forest after a member of the neighborhood grew dreadfully concerned upon seeing teenagers ambling into the woods, frightened to the point of evoking Johnny Law. And in this town, kids in the woods might as well be a serial killer at large, judging from the turnout the call would yield.

Arka pressed on, grateful this night hadn't yet proven such a case. Whatever beset them at the pits hadn't given way to a strobe of red and blue clawing through the widespread entanglement of trees. Obviously, something had spooked them proper, but he didn't think it was the pigs. It had to be rednecks, hunters; but at this hour? It didn't make sense. The most troubling issue at hand was the stint of amnesia, though it remained futile to devote it any concern. Memories would return in time.

He stopped and wondered if it might be better if it had been hunters. If the lights in the clearing were indeed some hallucination, then why the spontaneous communal panic? And why had they been so disorganized about it? He couldn't help but feel embarrassed over their conduct.

"No matter," he solemnly said. He could see Katrina's house perched atop the shallow hill and, with it, the dim lights of the following street. Arka was relieved to find the faint red glow emitting from the basement window as he deftly made his way up the small escarpment, crouching down beside the glass.

The television was on, producing a low murmur of indiscernible chatter. Katrina was no doubt watching some late-night pop-culture garbage, filler she claimed to subject herself to when she "didn't want to think."

Ah, the slow motion surrender to the whims of what's put in the glass box, displaying what countless studies indicate the masses want to see. Entertainment, usually the easiest to dissect and digest, straightforward fodder fed in intervals between endless advertisements and obnoxious proposals. One can mute or ignore these commercials, but they still occur in your realm of perception and will be processed by the brain in some measure. These bold pitches are aimed at all multitudes of target audiences. They stem from the idolizing of the decadent and famous, despite their morals and personal views, from glorifying the pursuit of looking how society says you should. They peddle all sorts of concoctions, creams, and cures, shifting the minds of young women to believe beauty harps on face-paints and the size of their chests. They preach people should pursue money above all else in order to attain happiness and that weight loss can occur simply through diet plans and pills.

Television, a perverse art in the quest for production dominance, how to prey off those who subject themselves to relentless suggestions in the search for entertainment – and it's not going anywhere.

Arka brushed his aversion aside and gently rapped on the window, waiting for some response. Nothing. After a couple more attempts, he made his way down the recessed basement stairs to search about the cobweb-infested ceramic pot near the door.

Katrina had long been a dear friend. Although the boy's late-night campaigns cost her countless hours of lost sleep in spite of her education, which she actually cared about – a stark contrast to her frequenting refugees – she always invited the prospect of company. Arka gripped his quarry and brushed the loose soil off the dull silver, utilizing his nails to etch out what was caked in the key's grooves. He sighed and slid it into the doorknob.

"Open the door."

Arka tensed. The words were not his own. He threw his back against the door, clutching the knob tightly from behind. He hadn't heard that voice in years. It was the kind of hammer-fall that indicated significant trepidation was still ahead. Any experienced psycho-experimentalist knew these triggers usually occurred in waves. It was important not to panic. Arka's imperturbability was a point of self-pride. It had to be some trick, some strange inner mockery in the form of an auditory hallucination. He feverishly scanned what narrow field of vision was granted between the stairwell walls, seeing nothing amidst the yard above.

"Okay, steady," he whispered. The voice had kicked up his heart rate and he was breathing heavy. He slowly turned the doorknob and backed into the dark of the basement, closing the door behind him.

Arka had become so acclimated to the wind that he now observed a daunting silence brought on by the foreboding lack of perception. The television? Not even. He made his way over to the bedroom door and carefully pushed it open, spilling the soft red light into the basement hall. He entered and found Katrina decidedly absent, allowing the following inclination of disappointment to pass as he reevaluated his situation.

The glare of the TV caught his eye and he took a step back from the images moving about the screen. Displayed were the backs of three men walking down a dimly lit road. They carried themselves in a familiar manner, as if it were an eerie recording of himself and his friends, only with shorter hair traveling down some foreign road. They were heading toward a white light. As Arka focused, it grew brighter until its radiance overcame the restrictions of the glass and left the edges of the television, creeping out onto the walls of the room. Arka stood in center-space, and was swallowed by it.

He found himself standing in a whitened room. The familiar outlines of Katrina's bed, dresser, shelves, the TV, and anything else recognizable were gone. There was but a single window to his left and a door straight ahead. He braced himself and positioned his arms toward his chest, readying his guard for whatever madness was sure to present itself.

It was now obvious he must be dreaming. Though the Runners thankfully considered themselves of superior proficiency when it came to dispatching nightmares, only after years of practice sleeping subsequent psycho-actives. The prevailing rule to heed was to remain steadfast and brave, confident and collected. Becoming terrified and irrational would only serve to compound the horror; should one play their emotions right, they may find themselves conquering the experience in debonair fashion.

Arka recalled his brother's extensive studies on the matter. Atris was knowledgeable and well-versed in nightmares as he had done the most digging into the field, although it was not his lasting intent. Several reckless months saw the development of a paranoid state of perpetual delusion, outright restricting his ability to sleep if the sun was not rising into the sky.

It wasn't some standard juvenile fear of the dark, described instead as something much more complex and menacing. It was as if something deep within him lost trust in the routine remission of his consciousness, unable to warrant rest while darkness or even faux light held sway on his surroundings. Should such a mistake come to pass, he would fall into an exceedingly lucid and painful experience. It was only after training his conscious mind to attain realization during sleep, grab hold of the situation and his faltering ego, and commit to defeating whatever affliction came his way that this stretch of mania was made to pass.

The underlying procedure carried into waking life as well, only the act of grasping the situation was far more drawn out, on a grander scale, and definitely never as interesting. After all, dreams are our mind's compensation for the predictability of the conscious hours spent in the physical world. Arka paused as he found this notion ironic. That was the twisted goal behind everything going on right now, perhaps the principal motivation fueling all their exploits: Drugs bring dreams to the waking world. It was an excessive assault on said predictability and rigid physical limitations. It was a silent war they were waging, one without a tangible enemy, devoid of any gauge of loss or gain, no score on the books. All other outlets for release were going stale or extinct. There were no natural enemies left, no targets to channel aggression and the mounting desire to punch something in the face. Even retaliation against contemporary bullying had been criminalized, with cops incessantly roaming high-school halls, wrenching down the seal on the defiant teenager trying to find some means to break free in a world going soft.

Arka stood resolute, concentrating on the next move. He found it strange nothing had happened yet, though comforting he was at least in control of his own conscious direction. He took a few steps forward and opened the door.

The settings around him proved foreign, though more inviting than a dark, musty basement with the horrid odor of cat litter. There was a hallway running left to right, with burgundy carpet lining up to the walls, covering the wood floor now creaking beneath his feet.

Arka headed to the right, ever cautious yet confident, despite how real everything around him felt. He could feel the draft sweeping down the hall and smell the nylon fibers that made up the rug. His eyes strained and adjusted to the dim light of the repeating flame-lit lamps hanging every ten feet or so. The curtains on the few recurring windows danced effortlessly on the cool air coming from outside, whipping sporadic curls of white light into the hall to overwhelm the inferior orange within. These high levels of perception came off rather odd indeed. No worries though, he had this one.

★★★★

Ewan was lost. The winding road slowly validated this growing suspicion. He discerned he must now be on a back road in a neighborhood the next town over. He was impressed for a moment, having apparently covered a considerable distance during the escape, though this gave way to irritancy after he wholly admitted to himself there were no familiar points to pull from.

Normally, he would've found comfort in discovering a new area, but being alone and still shaken from the accounts at the pits, no bright side was shed. He finally came to an intersection and looked around. The street sign appeared to have been pilfered, no doubt now currently adorning the bedroom wall of a nearby teenager.

This annoyed Ewan to a point, but he couldn't stay pissed.

He laughed to himself, recalling transients slowly rolling through Runner turf, halting at every corner since stripped of its labels, attempting to regain orientation after losing their way at the boy's hands. The practice had since lost its flavor these days, seeing as how damn near everyone had those GPS deals. Ewan and his peers were another middle generation of technology. They catalogued lasting memories of doorbells and landlines, in similar fashion of those who witnessed the proliferation of automobiles, airplanes, and television. Now the gap had been bridged via the internet and the smartphone, and any visual or auditory stimulation was a mouse-click or iPod shuffle away. Society now wallowed in a paradox of being more connected than ever while simultaneously disconnecting from physical interactions and confrontation. Everything's easier in text messages and e-mails, right?

Ewan shrugged off the thought and chose the leftward path. He was pleased to see homes come into view as he voyaged on, even though they boasted no real signs of life. It felt like he had been on the empty road for an eternity. He kicked a rock and sent it skidding over the asphalt river, hating when such notions crossed his mind. Forever was a long damn time; nothing should last that long.

Four figures appeared up ahead.

He considered fleeing, then thought better of it. *It'd look more suspicious if you turned and went back the way you came. Maybe up the hood though.* Ewan could hear them heatedly discussing something, though he was more concerned with slipping by unopposed than eavesdropping. He passed them without incident, without making eye contact or getting a good look at their faces, and began to put some distance between them.

"Yeah, but it hasn't even started yet." A strangely familiar voice spoke distinctly above the earlier whispers.

"It's takin' forever," another answered.

Ewan almost turned around, barely restraining himself from confronting whoever would say such a thing at a time like this. Small coincidences of the like were solid clicks up the roller coaster track.

"About time." A third voice spoke as Ewan moved further away. Composing himself and unclenching his fists, he continued onward and laughed slightly, ever fending off the tension.

The next street was a four-way intersection, with a small church gracing the right side. It was a quaint structure, with a modest yard and a small cemetery behind it. Truthfully, he never thought much on the prospect of death. Maybe it was the sight of the deer earlier or the proximity of the graveyard that provoked its unusual prominence in his thoughts. Death was a concept in which everyone around that age had to land on some sort of loose opinion.

Akin to most challenges of the future however, there was no point in dwelling on such things in excess, especially this matter most unknown. He couldn't apply the formula with death, the commonplace examination the boys tried to put to all their experiences. In order to form any solid opinion about anything – or anyone for that matter – they had to strictly experience it first-hand. Sure, he could trust the outlooks of his close friends, but to be one-hundred percent on something, the only way to do it was to undergo the trial personally.

The low hum of his phone suddenly could be heard as it vibrated against his outer thigh. His earlier attempts to reach Atris since they separated had been unsuccessful. Atris was an asshole like that, always finding small ways to spin things so they became problematic. He'd just decide to go a day without his phone entirely. He even got rid of his gaming consoles because he felt they'd become a waste of time and decisive distractions from his goals. Ewan wasn't sure how these experiments were accomplishing anything besides erecting needless barriers against the simple comforts of modern convenience – the very comforts that might prove invaluable on nights when they all got lost in the woods for example.

His phone gently pulsed once more, and he pulled it from his pocket. At least now he'd have someone to talk to. The small light-blue screen displayed the word "Unknown" as it droned a third time. Ah, many times before had he been duped upon risking such connection and actually answering a blocked number. It was a hard choice to make, as picking up could either alleviate his predicament or compound it. Ewan sighed and looked about as the wind rose and lulled. He flipped the phone open and brought it to his ear.

"Hello?"

"Hey, man." The voice was foreign, though absent any menace.

"What's up?"

"Heard you were on the run."

Ewan was both intrigued and immediately annoyed.

"Uh, no actually, just hanging out. Who's this?" He was in no mood for games. There was no answer from the other end. A light was coming up on Ewan's position, and he was forced to take shelter among the trees of the small graveyard. The line cut out as the car passed. *Great, what a bunch of assholes.* He was lost, and his friends were taunting him. He waited a minute for a call back and did his best not to become enraged, once more trying to raise Atris and failing yet again.

He heard the faint sound of footsteps heading his way and climbed around to the backside entrance of a crypt to avoid being seen from the street. The four figures from earlier were in full sprint, flying down the road, undeniably running from some pronounced peril. Much to his dismay, Ewan's best option was to sulk down beside the door of the crypt.

Suddenly, there were lights all about the road. The same luminescence that had ailed them at the pits, he was sure of it. He turned to the aged iron door but quickly decided he'd rather run then hide in some tomb, waiting to be snagged by zombies. He assessed alternatives.

The woods around these parts were too thick to dash through, too riddled with thorns and undetectable marshlands. If the assailants saw him make a break for a swamp, he'd be as good as surrounded, and definitely soaked. Bad nights. Though there was still some time to move in this case. He took after the four strangers and did his best to get his breathing rhythm right.

The light came from out of nowhere. No later than getting his foot off to the side in attempt to make for the woods was it instantly upon him, and became all he could see.

He felt like floating.

4

The beginnings will meet where all of this ends
the players in part, cut back from the start
and hold their lanterns against the web of the all.
We'll take in everything we know
what's been taught, what's been sown
and play the whispers rise
as the collective voice unfurls the story of our lives.

Atris's vision vied for focus. He found himself lying upon a soft surface, and slowly sat up to scan the room for any indication as to his new location. The flickering light overhead revealed only a couple chairs and a door nearby. He rolled off the bed to let his boots stain the pale-white floor as he moved toward the chair he had seen Aislin in. His thoughts caught up with him.

Well, we've finally broken through the rift.

It was safe to assume he was dealing with matters within himself, a lucid dream-state maybe. He could only hope his body was safe elsewhere.

He'd probably passed out beneath a tree. At least he'd now press on without worry of malevolent externalities, for ahead lay far different threats, hazards of the psyche. This mess had to be turned around. He would look at it with excitement even, an eloquent path toward some discovery, however bold or menial it might ultimately prove.

Opening the door, he set foot into a courtyard boasting numerous hedges and a few scattered trees. The structure bordered the yard on three sides, in a sort of horseshoe fashion, with the exempt wall giving way to a sheer drop. The sky was overcast, and the small amount of light from behind the clouds played on a blanketing fog that stretched straight to the horizon. Atris carefully made his way along a cobblestone path, into the center of the yard. The walls were of white stone and stood two stories high. The abundant windows on the upper level were all ajar as a gentle breeze came up the cliff and ran through their curtains.

"You know, it's probably dangerous to wander this place alone." The stern, confident voice seemed to come from every corner of the yard, echoing off the ivory walls. Atris stood his ground and scanned the brush for anyone, anything. He wished he had somehow armed himself before leaving the room.

"What's so dangerous about it?"

There was a long pause before a response came through the thickening fog.

"You know what lies ahead. You've been there before." The voice amplified as Atris fought to steady his heart. Whoever spoke was likely getting at a desperate cerebral inner-recess, a state of anguish and despondency, coupled with complete decimation of the ego and all other votes of self-confidence.

It wasn't justifiable to call it hell, but on a very personal level, it was an accurate enough word for it. Twice before Atris had been subject to this seemingly endless mental loop, certain he had died, forced to endure primal dread and hopelessness as apparitions of those he loved faded in and out about him. All the while, a searing sensation emanating at the core of his mind. There was no comprehension of time there. It had been replaced with certainty that madness would continue on for eternity.

"Nope. Not going back." Atris reassured himself and raised his guard, his hoodie flying wildly about his sides. It was important not to get too worked up, though more crucial still was to never lose courage, to take on any foe, whether he could see him, her, it – whatever – or not. This was all in his head, and could therefore be conquered via the correct approach.

He recalled his own writings on the matter.

The first mechanism, as he had dubbed it, was a fear trigger that implemented the prospect he had left his body and it might be too late to ever get back. This paranoia would snowball to crushing caliber and terminate the ego. It'd render an individual interpretation of the very worst of possibilities. The flailing mind would tap into a primal sense of fear and take all learned notions of labeled hell to forge terrifyingly personal manifestations, drastically launching the mind and body into a harrowing frenzy as they scrambled to attain oneness again. He reconciled his recounting with the situation before him.

"Come on out!"

He received no answer. The walls of the structure began to shake and he rushed to the door, kicking it open to barrel back into the white room.

"Right then. Never gonna take us." He grabbed one of the chairs and furiously flung it against the wall. It split in all the right places, and he pried off two of the legs, taking note of the rather spot-on carpentry before running out of the room once again. He made his way along the confines of the yard, brushing aside the low-hanging braches that seemed to descend on him from every direction.

Smashing a low window with the makeshift club, Atris dove inside the building. He heard another window crash from around the corner to the right. The building must instead be in some sort of "H" arrangement, as the hallway stretched much further than he'd anticipated. The shaking slowed and the structure steadied.

Clamoring to his feet amongst the shards of glass, he darted across the corridor and made for the first door he saw in the wall opposite the yard. He turned the knob and stepped inside a sizable foyer.

This was more like it. The faint smell of a fireplace filled the air, and the windows on the far side presented the magnificent resonance of a recent sunset.

There were a few bookshelves to the left, with an end table between two elegant chairs. Atris made his way across the royal-blue carpet and sat facing the fireplace. He sank low in the chair and brought his hand to his side, ensuring that his pen had made it with him to this foreign place.

Should he just wait for someone? For something? He must preserve a balance between aggression and patience, though it was also important to stay on the move. Whatever harbinger of the other side was encountered in the courtyard must be confronted sooner or later. He couldn't hide in some place that only existed in his mind. One way or another, he'd find himself.

Atris nearly laughed in spite of this thought, but he heard the gentle turn of the doorknob and leapt from his seat, wielding the improvised club as the door opened. Arka shuffled into the room.

"Oi, brother!" Atris's heart relaxed as he fell back into the chair. Arka studied the area for a moment before walking over and sitting down beside him.

"Right. So you really here?" Arka faced Atris inquisitively.

This question was decidedly not as senseless as it first came off, held in the same manner as asking an undercover narc if they were a cop or not. They had to answer truthfully, or else – come to think of it, or else what? They could just as easily deny the lie later. No matter.

"I feel real," Atris said, scratching the back of his head. "Here, have a chair leg." Arka received the piece of wood and felt about the nail protruding out its broader end, as if seeking some clarifying sensation of pain.

"Sweet. So what do you make of this? And what of the pits earlier?"

Atris shifted in the chair to look out the window as the last lit wisp of clouds gave way to darkness. "Well, the lights have to be some powerful result of the dose. We're all probably still at the pits, lying by the fire; which might account for that." He motioned toward the calm fireplace with the chair leg. "What's rather strange is the undeniable lucidity of this trip, along with complete voluntary control. It's not like anything I remember before."

Arka nodded. "I went to Katrina's after we split. She wasn't there, but someone else was. At first I thought someone might be having us on, but this place destroys that theory." He glanced at the ceiling and the chandelier hanging overhead.

"Maybe the others are somewhere around here," Atris said hopefully.

"Yeah, who knows?" Arka shrugged. "Have to look at it from the best of standpoints, and ride this thing back out to the other side."

Atris nodded toward the door. "Wait, did you break a window too?"

"No, got swallowed by the TV, then walked down a couple halls to get here."

"Right." Atris stood. "Someone else might be wandering the building. Shall we?"

Arka stretched. "Why not wait here? It's comfortable at least."

"Yeah, but we ought to see if Ewan and Aislin need–" The ground started shaking again. Arka grabbed the arms of his chair, as if to steady the floor by means of his own weight and will. His efforts actually seemed to work, and the chandelier above them swayed once more to static suspension, its crystal drippings rendering eerie rhythms in resonate tones.

"Right," he scoffed, turning to Atris. "Let's do it."

They made their way to the exit.

"Hey, you get the feeling you've been here before?" Arka was curious.

"Don't even." Atris kicked open the heavy door. It swung wildly, crashing against the wall.

Arka strode confidently through the opening, as if trying to convince himself he somehow knew the way.

Atris followed.

"Look on the bright side. This may turn out to be quite the story."

Atris tended to be concerned with things like that, often to the point of outwardly unnerving Arka. It was always a drastic move or an ill-advised play, after consideration and subsequent discarding of any threats in consequence. Atris was a man of stories, of being remembered, while still not caring about being revered. It was a result of his restless way of life. At that point, as far as they could figure, the only way to live was to do so to the fullest extent possible, and any other course was simply surrender in disguise, in whatever form one chose.

Indeed, the definition of said "full extent" continuously warped and shifted throughout the years, the pursuit of life's simpler pleasures taking a backseat for the rising worries of oncoming adulthood. Whatever the objective, the boys would deliver in a reckless manner often scrutinized by many, though it came off as Beethoven to them – grand demonstrations of true wayward will and steadfast grit in the face of the varying evils at work in the world.

The true question was a matter of possessing the rigid devotion required. The roads ahead were littered with parasites and the encampments of those who hadn't the heart to travel any further. Though the destination might be unclear, all that mattered was to keep going and never hit that point of surrender. Never stop, always believe matters could improve, and consistently strive to see it so. As soon as they doubted themselves, the walls would come down.

Arka had always been quick to highlight the irrationality of his brother's decisions, in Atris's damning of logical parameters. The risks were often of daunting caliber and not worth potential outcomes, leading to select journeys being written off from the start. Ewan and Atris were continually all for the fight, considering themselves indestructible until the wolves were closing in. Arka would sit those few exploits out, his more sensible approach of erring on the side of caution rendering him the only one who managed to evade an arrest record.

Atris simply considered the no-holds-barred approach to be a prerequisite of a Runner, indicative of the lives they chose. School days were allotted for rest and recuperation between adventures, buffer zones between what glories the weekends could hold. And the potential was always there. It was merely a question of scale and opportunity.

They also prided themselves on being men of their word. In life, it was oftentimes all they had, and over the years it became apparent that the path of the righteous man was rooted in devout veracity. Many people they met along the way found it easier to fabricate achievements, boasting falsehoods for sake of procuring ego, standing, women, or whatever. These deceivers would harness lies to fashion false esteem with none of the risk or effort. Nothing genuine, nothing earned. Assholes, and their peer-base was rife with 'em.

Other than business transactions, a few parties here and there, and the occasional exception, the Runners kept matters and monuments within a strict inner circle; a practice they followed out of necessity. Certain outside groups would occasionally emerge, integrate, and be barred in time. This was mostly due to a lacking of the paramount factor required in any lasting relationship: trust.

When matters turn dire, when the chips are down, one has to know exactly who they are standing next to. Each must know the other's mind, what they're capable of, and that they see each other in the same light. That was the only way the Runners worked so closely together for so long. It was the only way they figured best friends should operate; a molding of personalities, each one respecting, learning, and compensating for the strengths and shortcomings of the others. Over time, it became evident this wasn't how other bands operated, and that kind of trust and conviction was of rare claim indeed.

It was this very trust that was now called into play. It resonated and stretched to the walls as the two brothers proceeded to the far end of the building. Their suspicions concerning the riveting detail and shared lucidity were worrisome at first, though soon a sense of amazement began to overtake them as an ember brooding in the coal bed. Previous undertones of doubt and anxiety diminished through means of reliable company. The boys believed this kind of test had the potential to bring them to some magnificent epiphany, to the point of it all, even if they weren't sure what it might be yet.

5

By moonlight, the transients find respite to shuffle through this bitter night,
tomorrow we'll join the ranks of the listless who fight to remain.
on this asphalt here, do we abstain from view
all the lights far off to strangle few
wager-alls, short stops, and frequent falls have trapped us here in the halls within.
There's a war in the future to tear out the sutures of our generation
but where will it begin?

Ewan removed another shard of glass from his pant leg and sunk low in the chair, warming himself by the fire. He was thoroughly distraught upon being taken off the road by – well, something – and flung through a window the next second later. He couldn't end up in the middle of a stretching green field with the wind on his face or on a sun-kissed beach of white sand. No, the path he had been set upon had to lead him into plate glass. These aliens sure had a sense of humor. At least he wasn't cut.

He wondered if this might somehow be the doing of the four figures he had tailed before the lights got him, or if they – or members of his own group, for that matter – were somewhere around this wretched building as well. It was nearly dark outside, and his current comforts proved insufficient to keep frustration at bay. Why was this happening?

No, don't lose your head. He jumped up from the armchair and walked across the soft sky-blue carpet to a remarkable span of shelves. He had taken refuge in a narrow study of sorts, with subtle décor and a single armchair smelling of fresh pine facing the shelves. A good read was among the last of his current priorities, but any room with one entrance and four solid walls would do for the time being.

He regained his breath and revisited previous events, conceiving no stretch of an explanation as to how he got to this place. Instead, he moved to wonder *why* he might be there. Ewan often had to deal with a complete lack of causality. It was a downright luxury at times. Admittedly, this also proved a twisted motivation for their ventures. With growing frequency and feverish intensity, he and his band often found themselves in tight trials and battles of the mind. The warped thrill of it all kept them coming back. Traditional motives of mere amusement had long since given way to more complex, reputable channels of self-discovery and – who knows? – maybe eventual audience with a higher consciousness.

Yeah, right.

All partakers of the counterculture had their own reasons, methods, and morals. Variation amongst users was vast, the gamut far too wide to allow any classifying into general collectives. Still, society's rigid judgments saw fit to do just that, dismissively branding everyone together as misguided fiends.

Most users did it strictly for entertainment, chasing fleeting happiness in many forms, a fundamental pursuit one couldn't stack much argument against. Others did it to rid themselves of guilt and worry, however temporary the relief might be. Further down the spectrum, mostly in the domain of opiates, were those deeming dosage necessary, under banner of hopeless addiction – an approach fueled of selfish drive and mere physical pleasure while retarding the mind, dulling the senses, and restricting any real growth. These were shallow measures the Runners dubbed obvious wastes of energy and time.

Drugs were often utilized as means to combat boredom when there was simply nothing else on a day's agenda. This tended to result in blind habit in lieu of hobby. Overindulgence was a dangerous behavior, and the boys were avid proponents in the prospect of too much of a good thing. They looked on such approaches with underlying disdain. It made them look bad and went against their own set of objectives. Atris would firmly justify use as a tool, an extension of his fingertips even, akin with his pen. Sure, their intentions would always involve entertainment, though it was avant-garde exploration that took center stage as the years turned, a means of spiritual study even.

Their kind were always in the game for adventure, the good and the bad. They were after results. Should boredom be designated foe, they resolved to see it dispatched in a more savage manner, yielding greater stories and brighter memories. As far as the boys were concerned, it was in this way they would rise above the rest. The difference was simply hidden in the breakdown of the aforementioned speculations; most other travelers of the mind got done by drugs. They were the ones who did drugs, and they considered themselves prodigious masters of the twisted art.

In truth, it hadn't been just about having a good time for a long while now. Ewan thought it might even be about this very plight. Such accountings and mission statements were usually left to Atris, ever-driven by some need to write everything down in those books of his. Ewan had always found himself paging through only scattered dates, humorous quotes, and other assorted nonsense, with Atris's own scripture and prose intertwined into strange poetry. Perhaps he had hoped to bridge the gap between his conscious self and that of his sub somewhere along the way. Yeah, Atris would find this room fascinating for sure.

Ewan moved to browse the literature displayed before him, calming himself with the notion of discovery. He removed a random work from the shelf and gently parted its bindings. To his surprise, there was indeed legible writing:

From time to time, it is only human one may face a restlessness of spirit, a doubt of worth, or absent meaning. There are no certain answers for questions concerning existence after death or the reason behind life. We are afforded faith and tend to believe the universe to possess some degree of order, yet ultimately these mysteries remain. We are given great stories to elicit wonder, entice possibility, and to examine these questions of the human condition.

As the variable traveler may follow the model of the mythic king of old, so might his own footprints in the sand be found by others; shipwrecked brothers and free hearts alike. And where his own temporal markings on the shores of the years may be erased in an instant on the whims of the wind, it is the fight and not the outcome that counts in the end.

Ewan reflected on the last sentence. Atris would always harp on some great struggle they were apparently involved in, sometimes even on the most carefree of summer nights. He came off ever-restless, over-analytical, and anxious. The words might as well be his if in fact they weren't.

Ewan closed the pages and continued his search for pertinent information. Another selection contained a logbook of some sort:

November?

I can't begin to figure out how long I've been here. Thankfully, I still have these pages to compile some sort of account, as if there is much to record.

The actions I take now may restrict my return to this place, though I figure there is nothing keeping me here. At tomorrow's first light I'll head in the direction of the – well whatever mimelight mocks the sun behind all these clouds. I would very much like to feel its warmth once more ... wonder when I'll wake up.

Ewan shuddered as he digested the entry. The written words in front of him started to trail off the paper. Angered, he quickly turned the page.

All right, concentrate.

Concentration, in and of itself, always proved challenging for him. Focus on the task at hand was only made possible after all measures of distraction were thoroughly done away with. Most people these days called it attention deficit disorder. But when and why exactly did society start giving labels to natural afflictions of a developing mind – labels containing the words "disorder," "disease," or "deficiency"?

The answer was simple, Ewan decided. The very same answer to ninety-five percent of all questions ever asked: money.

Sure, it all started out in the name of scientific achievement, to make life better for those with "disorders." Though decades down the line, the landslide result became parents everywhere scrambling for widespread medications for Johnny and Jane, who weren't simply tired or apathetic toward their class subjects, but were instead suffering from chemical imbalances that needed to be rectified if they were going to make it in the world. And the whole "concentrating disease" was just the most popular ailment affecting the youth around them.

Then there were the anxiety disorders, paranoid delusions, schizophrenia – all the big-name heavy hitters that were self-reinforcing stamps on the impressionable foreheads of the modern teen, most of which simply needed some solid friendship and aid, but instead received a prescription bottle along with a handicap to hold onto, embrace, and cultivate. The boys had seen it many times before. But what did they know anyway? They weren't the ones with the PhDs.

Ewan shrugged in spite of himself.

He was fairly certain the RX Empire of America was just another case of natural selection taking the back seat in the evolution game. He figured a few years down the line they would all be prescribed to something or another. Shit, they already were. Pretty soon there would be a pill or an injection to drastically slow aging. Then over the next century or so, the world could continue to overpopulate and fill to the brim. Countries would vie for more territory to compensate for booming populations and we could hurry along with this nuclear Armageddon deal. Why not?

He grasped the book tighter and slammed it into his forehead as the words came back into focus:

December?

Act 1: Everything under the one. It's another voyage, possibly one of the last with this crew of three. Each of us ready, seasoned veterans of the sea.

The rain that slowly falls from above relays the calls of those that fly ahead of us.

The sky is a must.

A sustained shade of blue, across the traces of mountainous gain

From the fields we will sustain

It's time to fly boys, out into the mind.

It's our time to try boys, our hand at levity once more.

Only blank pages followed after that. Ewan returned the ledger to its recess and proceeded further down the line:

An Understanding of Antipodes

Daily Inspection Cards for F/A-18E

Passwords for Levels of "Megaman X"

Fire and Its Tendencies

Hand Soap, an Essay

A Manual on Industrial-strength Dishwashers

A Brief History of Argentina

Each cover presented something more arbitrary and less helpful than the last. There were still plenty of others to check, but Ewan was growing impatient.

At least this dude had plenty to read. He turned and made his way to the door, throwing out his chest and clenching his fists, as if posturing himself for a brawl of sorts. He remembered Atris had once criticized this manner of walking, claiming his superior method of clasping one wrist behind his back was the best form to put oneself into the wind and absorb life. Ewan laughed at the thought as he turned the handle and pulled the door open.

He was looking at himself, a complete copy of his likeness, only garbed in slightly more snug attire, staring back at him with a somewhat venerable expression.

Ewan quickly slammed the door and took off for the far corner of the room, intent on wielding books as projectiles against the imposter.

Nothing happened. The door didn't open, but he could swear he heard footsteps fade away from beyond it.

A minute passed before he cautiously made his way over for a second exit attempt, turning the handle and wildly leaping into the hall. There was a figure down a ways and to the right.

"Ewan, that you?" Arka's semblance came into the faint light of the lamps hanging from the walls.

Ewan sighed relief and shut the door behind him.

"Dude, what is going on around here!?" He met Arka and was subsequently taken aback by his appearance. His face seemed to have aged, and his hair was cut exceedingly short, nowhere near its usual length. In turn, Arka seemed less alarmed with Ewan, allowing only a slight hint of surprise to surface on his face.

"You look different." Ewan's hesitant voice bore apprehension. He was unwilling to concede comfort in the meeting of his friend, who had already started down the hall.

"Never mind that," Arka said over his shoulder. "We have to keep moving if we are to get out of here and find the others." He paused for a moment, allowing Ewan ample time to brush rising uneasiness aside and continue after him.

The lights dimmed, and the walls groaned beneath some sort of unseen weight before slowly starting to close in on them.

"Move!" Arka shouted, bounding into a full sprint. They raced down the hall toward a faint glow beyond a mess of rubble, apparently remnants of the far wall. The duo flew out of the opening, rolling onto the soft grass of a dark field. The horrible groan that resounded about them came to a peak and the terrain shook violently, spewing a billow of soil out of the ground to blanket the area.

Ewan remained still for a moment before flinging up in sporadic fashion and winging around to free himself of the ensuing layer of dirt. Arka was on his feet and brushing himself off.

Ewan coughed. "Shit!" The structure was gone, as if it'd never been there in the first place.

"I didn't think..." Arka started.

"Damn! What the hell is next?" Ewan asked.

Arka turned to face him. There was a gradual downgrade on the hill to a low plain, and the light from the sky revealed some disturbance frantically moving away through the high grass. It was impossible to discern if it was but a single being or several in flight.

"It was you that passed us before, wasn't it?" Arka calmly inquired.

Ewan scowled, wearing blatant confusion. "What?"

Arka finished removing the dirt from his shoulders. "On the road. You went straight by us, right?"

Ewan recoiled at the question rephrased. "What are you talking about?"

"Earlier, when we ran from the lights."

Ewan still didn't signal any connection.

"We've been here before. Things sure seem to be falling apart at a fast rate though." Arka's first words came confident, though his last statement carried marked concern. "Listen, if you are the first time, then we gotta get this straightened out first."

"What do you mean 'the first time'?" Ewan's pulse quickened, suddenly doubting if Arka was even himself and not some malevolent force made familiar illusion.

"You see, we keep coming back, looking for answers." Arka took his hands out of his pockets, reluctantly resigning his search for a cigarette. "The problem is we always end up running out of time before we get any closer, and what we've achieved is lost. We can't remember." He gazed up into the bright sky.

Ewan followed his glance, fending off agitation.

The moon proved a solid white disc, devoid of typical lunar features, most notably the dark indentations of the Sea of Tranquility or the standalone Mare Carius. A gigantic, faint ring of light circled it some three feet around as the naked eye could perceive. Ewan had seen it before, but couldn't remember when.

"Regardless, we have to make it to the tower before sunrise. Otherwise, we might be trapped." Arka started off down the hill.

Ewan cautiously followed.

"You're telling me you've been here before and there's a chance of us getting stuck?"

"Yes, but it was a younger self that led to me." Arka explained, rubbing his neck.

"All right, so let me put this together. You and the three others I saw on the road are all in here with us. And you're all older copies?"

"Copies, well not necessarily; we are each other, just further down the line. Still trying to uncover what we need to find." Arka slowed as they reached the base of the hill, then pushed onward through the low grass as the plain leveled out.

"So, sunrise," Ewan said. "We gotta be at some tower. Or else, bad shit?" He decided not to delve further into the inquisition.

Arka glanced back at him. "You're taking this better than I thought you would. There's no need to worry, we'll make it. There should be plenty of time left."

"Right, as long as you know what you're doing. Where is everyone else then?" Ewan couldn't shake the sense of worry still contending for prominence in his conduct.

"Probably ahead of us. Reckon we always make it out of the cliff house in time." Arka paused. "But you didn't count on seeing yourself, so I figured I would head back for you before the place came down. ... Though, I didn't expect it to—"

"How do you know so much if you can't remember the other times?" Ewan was trying his best to even out the level of trust with this familiar stranger.

"That's what the libraries are for, man. Everything you need, we wrote it in those books." Arka kept steady pace across the grassy plain. "You just have to kind of feel out which ones to select for the right information, before time is up. Kinda like life. The main archive is further ahead though, the structure beneath the tower."

"Main archive? There's a bigger stash of books?"

"Countless more." Arka seemed almost proud. "There's an immeasurable amount written between the seven of us."

"Seven?"

"Right. Well, that's the collective number as far as we can figure, from the ledgers we've found. We don't know how many times we've been here before, but we're pretty sure others have visited, maybe found their own ways out. I don't know why they aren't here with us now, but we believe it's just us five that keep coming back: us, Atris, Brac and Nico." Arka didn't have to look back to know Ewan didn't understand. How could he?

"I don't know how old you are at this point, but you haven't met those two yet. You will though. We've got to keep moving, make the most of our time."

Ewan stopped in his tracks, driving his frustration into the ground. "How do we even know what time it is here!? That's all Atris would ever talk about in tight spots like this."

"Yes, and it's important we find him – in time." Arka laughed and adjusted his tone to a different note. "Time is merely a man-made tool, a measuring device not concerned with whatever force put the sun and the moon into the sky. If things were as black and white as day and night we'd all go mad. Time is a gauge of how long we have to complete certain tasks set forth, how long until we must face an event or experience, how much further we label our age."

Arka was in danger of going into a lecture. "In its base analysis, time is just the period during which something exists or is in progress for. Though just like love, for example, it is impossible to really grasp the true, encompassing definition, or a proper understanding of it in so few words."

Arka paused to look back at Ewan and regain his composure. "And yes, there's no real perception of it here. As far as I figure, at one instance we all managed to meet up at the cliff house before venturing to the field beyond." He pointed upward. "The light resembling the moon there hangs in the sky for however long it wants to, until something triggers its descent. I can't remember what though. In short, it's been unanimously deemed the best course of action to make for the tower as soon as we can. We're deep in it now. Best not take any needless chances."

Ewan sneered, silently agreeing that it was in their favor to act. Further questions could wait. Undertones of dread passed with an ominous gust as the duo continued on their way.

6

Through you, beyond the worlds that knew you
hidden beneath the churning tide
time spent, whatever it meant
under skies of nurtured, gazing eyes
you taught me how to see, I taught you a different view
and our song echoed on in search of somewhere to belong.
For time wrought a cell, its balance measured well
lest chance and circumstance forge its metaphor for hell
And I can tell, yes, eye can tell.

B rac was in full sprint, madly dashing across barren terrain to escape the fog steadily rising from the nearby cliff edge. Maybe the lights were returning to take him out of whatever the hell he was in and move him elsewhere. Then again, maybe they weren't. Or perhaps the next place would boast obstacles far worse than base disorientation, fog, and the occasional ground-borne hand attempting to pull him into subterranean madness.

The lights remained the only thing he could remember. He was fairly certain there had been a road at some point, but the next thing he knew he was on this plateau, alone.

No more running. He slowed to a halt, the fog menacingly swirling around his ankles. He was of slender frame, taller than average with a devotion toward pushing the limits of everything he took on. Complete immersion in the challenge at hand yielded him an admirable reputation. He was known for his all-or-nothing attitude, which adhered seamlessly to Runner code.

Brac squinted through the fog.

"Nope, no point in staying still. Better keep moving."

He took to running again. The fog left an impression in his wake as if he were the famed coyote himself. Gazing up into the night sky, he observed points of light resembling stars slowly gliding to and fro, slow-motion comets stuck on some celestial circuit.

"Need more time!" The voice screaming into the heavens was barely his own.

Shit! He stopped in his tracks, skidding stones off into oblivion. He turned left and continued along the cliff at a steady pace, cautiously this time. As the orange gravel crunched underfoot, he continued to battle the mania that strengthened as he ran.

Keep running. You know this will save us in the end. It always has. Brac took some small reprieve from this self-assurance and steadied his heart. Running came naturally to all of them.

It was a base metaphor for life, for the fight. One must call upon form and focus to strive through the test, factoring in stride, cadence, and balance to push their body to proficiency. This orchestration must be kept flowing for as long as possible; whether it's flight from something or making the destination in time. The end biochemical result yields a healthy satisfaction impossible to mimic through any drug out there. The raw, physical act of running, under all its dissection is an allusion to a more complex practice. It was a prime representation of how they sought to live their lives, how to wage war.

Growing up, Brac and the others were always considered outsiders, consistently rebelling against decorum, questioning routine and combating the currents of public education.

From the moment they entered mainstream schooling, they were taught to keep quiet, to listen to the man at the front, to mimic the habits of the thirty peers around them while absorbing what the approved texts say; all the while accepting the information as pertinent to their lives. This was the way of things, and admittedly, they couldn't conceive any alternative method as efficient in dealing with the ever-increasing youth populace as a whole.

Though part of the whole was exactly what they weren't. The entire process was geared toward producing successful men and women to let loose into society, to uphold market structures and perpetuate cycles of supply and demand – to eat fast food, believe their votes counted, desire expensive cars, and stand in line on Black Friday. It was all developed in pursuit of money. In its simplest analysis, in the narrowest of assessments, success is money.

As adolescence went on, Brac and his company decided that wasn't the formula they'd utilize to achieve happiness. Their methods would be much more grand, more complex, passionate, and daring. The process couldn't be taught, it had to be felt; through hardship and heartache, blood and toxins, through the darkest of nights, and the very brightest days the masses wouldn't be able to comprehend. Brac wasn't certain how it was going to turn out. In fact, that was half their system's appeal. They didn't live this way for attention, entertainment, or to seek out others of similar mind. No, it was simply standard operating procedure. It came naturally, as it does with most wayward souls.

So throughout the years, when presented with tasks they wanted no part of, the boys would run, either physically or mentally. It was never out of cowardice or incompetence; it was in the hunt for something better. They ran because whatever was before them wasn't appealing and they weren't yet prepared to define sacrifice. There was no need for it in those days.

They lived life "in the now," damning all consequences, exchanging the promise of a stable future for the essence of freedom. Regular members of society don't want to be free. They want to be safe. They want insurance coverage, taxes to pay on a place to stay, a 401k, a steady current of currency, and the ability to provide for offspring. The acquisition and maintenance of true freedom was a dying art form, one not easily sustained. It took the right rhythm of a certain set of hearts and the very wildest of eyes.

Lost in his reflections, Brac had come to a halt. Noting the approaching fog, he suspected resuming his flight would simply bring him full circle, back into the rising cloud. Mounting terror was trying its best to smash through his mental levees and saturate his being. He sighed in contempt and remained steadfast, ready for the strange mist to engulf him.

Hopefully it wouldn't be as bad as he thought.

It came up on his position and formed his profile, cool at first but then gradually warming on the touch of his skin. His heart steadied and the paranoia began to subside. Of course, now he couldn't see a thing, and his sense of direction was exterminated. He sat to rest, careful not to sway too close to the drop off. The wind died. Complete silence was kept in check only by a low pitched, muffled whistling of sorts.

★★★★

It was like a far-off engine on the other side of a mountain, coming through in stereo, and it was all Atris and Arka could hear as they held tightly to the treetop, their highpoint of hope situating them above the imminent rubble. After roaming the white building and searching several rooms before the walls started to close around them, they'd raced back to the courtyard across shaking ground with the building leering down on the small garden.

There was no making it through; the enclosed yard afforded them the sole option of surviving the demolition by getting above it. They witnessed the structure jar and buckle, the second story collapsing into the first.

The ground gave way, and their perch rapidly became horizontal. Atris and Arka entered the low-lying fog and soon the renegade terrain smashed into the ocean. They lost sight of each other as they were launched through the air and into watery embrace. It enveloped them in cold darkness and broke their fall.

Atris recovered from the shock and kicked upward to the surface as small boulders crashed all around him.

"Arka! Ewan! Aislin!" He kept his head above the waves born of sporadic splashes.

Arka surfaced and coughed wildly to clear his lungs.

"Well," he wheezed before hacking up more water. "I guess that was one way to go." The structure was now half-submerged, along with massive portions of grass and mud. Atris treaded water for a moment and started laughing. They had ridden the landslide what appeared to be five or six stories down. He joined Arka and they both swam around the ruins, making for the small shoreline against the cliff. Moments later, the duo trudged out of the surf onto a rocky, driftwood-ridden beach.

Wet hoodies were removed and they proceeded to wring out their t-shirts as they surveyed the damage. The whole mess had settled in an encroachment on a thin coastline that stretched into the foggy veil, with the ocean at their backs rendering slight waves not of standard ebb. Perhaps the building landed in a large lake of sorts, though sighting any sign of the far coast was impossible. Fortunately, it seemed imminent danger had been left behind. The quake had ceased, and no failing construct threatened premature internment.

Atris lowered his vision to the cliff's face, noticing gigantic letters etched in the rocky escarpment, some five feet above their heads.

STEER CLEAR OF THE SE

The rest was buried beneath mud and debris.

Atris folded his arms, wet garbs in hand, as Arka walked up beside him.

"Right, so it's sticking to the coast then." Atris started off down the beach.

Arka quickly followed. "So how 'bout all that?"

"I felt for sure the adrenaline rush would've woken me up – and the blast of cold water. Though I guess we're deeper in it than that."

"This is something else, man," Arka discerned, observing the cliffs as they walked. The crags bore down closer to their level before shooting back up to original height, as if the jagged edge was some topographic taunt. "Sure hope we can find another way."

"Something tells me we will." Atris's voice was calm. The two proceeded down the coastline for a while before a sparkling light pierced through the haze. Cautious in their approach, they found a makeshift wooden dock beneath their feet, with the coastline thereafter narrowing sharply until it was one with the cliff face. The small dock appeared to have been damaged in the quake, though the water was considerably shallow at its far end. Several logs were strung together into a crude resemblance of a raft which bobbed up and down in the pseudo-tide, gently striking one of the boards comprising the pier. There seemed no alternative means of moving forward, and turning back certainly didn't feel right.

Arka motioned toward the raft. "After you, man."

Atris boarded the structure and shifted his weight around to test its integrity. He crouched down and lifted a thick, woven rope out of the water. It was anchored to the edge of the dock, ran through one of a few metal rings fastened to the raft, with the rest of it stretching off into the unknown, heading what they determined to be upstream. Atris seized tension of the rope while Arka procured the dock's single lantern and boarded the small vessel.

"Hope this'll lead back to higher ground." Atris heaved on the line in hand-over-hand fashion. "Being in the shadows of these cliffs is making me uneasy."

The raft skidded through the water in spurts with minimal effort, and the small pier was gradually put astern. Soon there was nothing save the calm sound of their shallow wake and the rope systematically rising in and out from the depths.

"How long do you think we were walking there?"

Arka shrugged. "Dunno, maybe ten minutes or so."

"Yeah, suppose it wasn't that long." Atris looked up at the moon and noticed it hadn't moved since he first saw it from the courtyard. He wondered what had become of Aislin and Ewan, if they'd made it out before the cliff gave way, had woken up, or weren't there in the first place.

"Don't worry about 'em." Arka looked up from the water's edge, as if sensing his friend's concern.

"Yeah, bet they found another way out." Atris reassured himself and continued to propel their raft upstream.

"Probably jumped out a window."

The bordering cliffs slowly appeared less-menacing as the river came to a bottleneck.

★★★★

"No sense of direction at all!" Brac was sitting cross-legged, trying his best not to let himself slip back into the bedlam he had risen above only moments before. The haze had since surrounded him and he tried to recall how he'd gotten to this accursed plateau.

"How is this possible? …isn't like any other dream I've felt before. There was a mission." He cupped his chin in one hand. "Of marked significance. Not just an ordinary journey. And the moon – there's something strange about it, something I've seen before. Before the sky started dividing."

The once-cooling touch of the fog had exceeded ambient temperature, escalating to humid discomfort. Brac stood and twisted around to stretch his back out. A small spark of hope took him as he spotted an orange glimmer cut through the fog from somewhere below, off the drop to his left. The low, muffled hum filling his ears was steadily overtaken by the gentle sound of flowing water, carried on a rising draft. And were those footsteps close by?

He didn't have long to evaluate matters. The humidity was definitely increasing, and he thought he felt sweat forming on his brow. And then the mist got worse, turning into hot steam.

"Ah hell." His whole body tensed and his stomach went into knots as the temperature around him continued to rise. Heat – one thing you didn't want in this game was inexplicably rising heat. Something was drastically wrong.

Brac backed against the ledge and quickly weighed his options, trying to think on some rational level. *All right, this is a bad trip, no doubt about it. I'm not really here. But then where am I?* He had no time left to pursue logic. It was a forsaken thing on this mesa of madness anyway.

"Shiiit!" Brac sprang from his footing, executing a corkscrew motion into the black of the night. The wind rushed by him, removing the scorching from his being, giving way to a low whistle rushing by his ears. He could feel his body cooling down. Now he could wake up.

Suddenly, he crashed into aquatic suspension, gratefully lulling in chill weightlessness for a spell before clawing to the surface. Treading water came easily, seeing as how there was only a slight current.

"Oi!"

He whirled around in the direction of the voice to see a small raft not thirty feet away.

"Yes!" Brac exclaimed and efficiently swam toward its position.

★★★★

Atris and Arka were suspicious of the stranger they had witnessed plummet from the high cliff, but believed it might've been Ewan or Aislin or maybe someone who knew what was going on. They agreed the risk of fishing a mental wanderer out of the river was well worth it. Atris stretched out his arm and helped Brac aboard.

"Damn, am I glad to see you," Brac started as he sprawled out on the deck, steadying his breath. "Burning fog up there. Where'd you guys get dumped?"

"Some unstable white building. What are you doing here?" Atris asked.

"I wish I knew, man. Can't remember for the life of me." Brac sat up and looked over at Arka. "Least I got company now. You guys build this crate?" He shifted his weight around, causing the vessel to sway.

Arka was confused. He had seen this newcomer before but failed to pinpoint exactly where or when it had been. He shied away from asking Atris how he came to know him. One of the schools they went to perhaps?

"Any idea what's going on?" he finally questioned.

Brac hesitated. He glanced around as if expecting some further strangeness to occur, before looking back at Arka.

"Told ya, can't remember. I thought I was with others but it seems I turned up alone. Did we come here together?" Arka found it evident Brac was genuinely trying to make sense of it all himself.

"Don't know, but its good we were here to pick you up," Atris said as he resumed pulling the raft through the water. "We're heading wherever the line is taking us."

"Hopefully, it's somewhere we'd want to go." Brac laughed as he moved to wring his shirt out into the river.

Arka sighed. "As long as it's somewhere." He remained wary of the stranger for the next few minutes, though there wasn't much opportunity to pry further regarding his involvement.

"Did you see that?" Brac gazed east, his arms folded. Arka stepped to his side, peering up at the rocky ledges. There was motion amidst the darkness, some trigger catching the lantern's low gleam, followed by splashes some hundred feet away.

"Another quake?" Atris asked.

"I don't think so, are those...?" Arka trailed off.

"Who would be?"

All three strained to make out the shapes of a few figures on the promontory before the raft shook, upsetting their focus. The wind returned abruptly and the river swelled. The boys crouched low, careful to allot their weight as inboard their small craft as possible.

"Here we go." Atris griped through clenched teeth and held onto the line. Arka was still trying to size up the nearby cliffs, feeling his temporary reprieve from hardship slipping away. Whitecaps sprouted up by the bluffs. The river churned and the boys found themselves unable to advance upstream.

"What do we do now?" Arka shouted, doing his best to shield their lantern from the surging wind.

"Take off your shirt!" Brac yelled back.

Arka hesitated. "Look, I'm flattered, but–"

Brac laughed, sprawling out to starboard and deftly tying one sleeve of his hoodie around the outboard log. The raft lurched and jolted violently, casting Atris backward onto the deck, limp towline in hand. Light vanished as the lantern was launched overboard.

7

The sea is swallowing the worries we've emitted
the eye is watching all of those acquitted-
an account of their cries, a record of their questions.
Waiting for a time, the answers we'll find-
buried in ourselves, sheltered in the mind
all fighting to uncover what's made us blind.
We've opened our eyes once more to the sky, striving to set aside ever asking why
for you never know when sparks will strike,
madness, beauty, and the like.

"So explain to me again, this whole copying deal?" Ewan couldn't help growing impatient as he kept up with Arka's swift pace across the grassy field.

His guide's words carried a certain agitation, "It's complicated. Just know there is basically an older you out there and that shit goes insane if you end up seein' 'em. Good thing you slammed the door on future-you back there. Better still, he walked away instead of investigating."

"That's not something I would've done," Ewan said indignantly. "Run away like that." Arka made sure Ewan understood how laughable he found such a statement.

"You wouldn't do something like that where you stand right now, maybe. But later on – well you just don't know how the tides of time will shape you. And if I were to guess, you're already closing in on the archives."

Ewan tried to remember the stare he saw in the doorway of the small library, his own eyes infiltrating his mind; a mirror image choking his concentration and accelerating his heart. He felt faint as they pressed across the plain. His head started pounding, and his own gaze steadily became all he could see.

★★★★

Ewan's legs were aching and his chest was tight, his lungs viciously fighting off years of abuse. Atris would always get all preachy about the whole smoking deal, labeling it a waste of money, energy, and to say the least, not worth damaging your lungs. You never know when you'll have to call on your stamina for a tussle or when zombies show up. Ewan always brushed such concerns aside, but now here he was, exhausted upon reaching the northern woods. He gave up his sprint at the tree line, pausing to lean against a large oak.

"Shit. Get ... a grip ... on yourself." His whispers were forced between staggered gasps for air. What a mess this trip had become already. He'd resolved to waste no time after he and the others had been consumed by the lights, immediately searching for one of the two cliff-house libraries. Ewan knew that intel from the start was of foremost concern in this place. And he had a feeling there was no time to spare standing around in awe, studying the ways, dissecting the whys, or attempting any form of construction.

He struck the mighty trunk in frustration. But of course, it was just his luck to find his younger variant barring entry into the library, somehow beat out by his rookie. He was always the one getting the raw deal, consistently compensating by way of his own strength, never a patron of fate. He was an avid proponent of making his own luck, as they say. It wasn't really that big of a deal. He remembered all the crucial facts, steadying his breathing as he reviewed them silently to himself:

Get to the tower, get to the lift, get ready for the others … just head north.

In keeping with his dismissive outlook on matters of fortune and coincidence, he believed he had an unmatched innate sense of direction and, furthermore, it was all he'd need. Sure, he had a hunch he and the others arrived for some purpose, perhaps searching for something, though after subduing the resulting trauma from seeing himself, he wasn't wasting any time trying to figure out what it was. They could reflect all they wanted once they were within sprinting distance of the exit.

Ewan turned and deftly made his way into the thick forest before him. Hopefully, there were only a few paths through the woods. He just had to keep his bearings, watch the sky, and head in the same direction he projected upon entering. Simple enough. He figured moss probably grew on the south face of tree trunks in dreams.

He'd only been walking for a few moments when he heard the loud snap of a tree branch from up ahead. The canopy above was thankfully not as dense as he'd feared, with ample moonlight penetrating the leaves to grace the forest floor and allow conservation of loose orientation. He had already committed to cover this darkness in full, and there wouldn't be enough time to turn around in hopes of seeking another way into the fog-ridden mountains ahead. There had to be a path to the far edge line, blazed via the right selections of the bifurcations ahead, leading straight to the rocky pass and up to the archives. Another twig sounded underfoot.

"Who's there?" A rough voice cut through the silence only to vanish as quickly as it had come.

A faint breeze slipped through the branches above, followed by the clamor from Ewan's new cover of a nearby bush. It was too dark. He couldn't see any movement.

"Brac?" The voice sounded again.

Ewan cleared his throat as quietly as he could. "No. Who're you?" He masked his normal tone.

A moment passed, and a few leaves were gently carried to the ground in the cradle of the wind.

"Nico."

Ewan sighed. "Great, it's you." He emerged from his cover and strode out to the trail to be met by a large, stocky character produced from the far side of the path. Ewan continued walking down the trail, barely heeding the newcomer's existence.

"Good to see you too." Nico scowled at Ewan's indifference as he followed after him. "It figures I would run into you. Feels like I've been wandering around here forever." His demeanor was calm and collected.

"There's that word again," Ewan muttered under his breath.

"Seen any of the others?" Nico asked as he caught up.

"No." Ewan didn't break stride. "We've got to get to the tower and get out of here. We've wasted too much time already."

"What time is it anyway?"

Ewan chuckled and glanced over his shoulder. "I don't know, man. Your phone's gone too, isn't it?"

"So what's the rush?" Nico inquired in turn, unfazed by his cohort's rising irritability. Ewan halted, spinning around wildly in attempt to discourage whatever follow-up questions his company had on deck.

"I saw someone," Nico began. "She was wandering through the trees. And there was a light, a dim aura of sorts, seemed to follow her as she went."

"Chick had a flashlight, good for her." Ewan folded his arms. "Must be nice."

"Just wondering if you've seen her."

"Nope. Maybe she's headed north and—" Ewan stopped short of his next word, as if only now giving Nico's quandary any real consideration. "I'd be real careful of what goes on in these woods, bro. You get that feeling that familiarity is all around you and yet you can't remember a thing either, can you?"

Nico shook his head. "But you have seen her then?"

"I haven't seen anyone 'sides yourself." Ewan turned from him, proceeding down the path. "Look, I'm going to need your help up ahead, big-man. We have to make sure the lift is working so we can get outta this place." Ewan was measuring the sky in a forlorn search for stars obscured by clouds when he noticed his wake was absent the sound of leaves trampled underfoot. He was alone once again.

"That figures," he started derisively. "Want something done right…"

★★★★

"Hey! ... Hey!" Arka's voice resonated in Ewan's head, slowly dissolving what seemed like plugs impeding his ears, as if he were rising to the surface of water. "Ewan!" His name vibrated above a low drawn-out hum. His vision widened from black, pushing back the narrow limitations of the immediate foreground and finally out to full peripheral field.

Arka was standing some feet away with a great chasm at his back, beside what appeared to be the start of a rope bridge. Ewan surprisingly found himself still standing, and this shock alone caused his legs to give out.

Arka walked over to him. "You haven't said anything in a while ... Not like you. Still with me?" He extended his hand to help Ewan to his feet.

"Yeah, right." Ewan's voice was uncertain as he rubbed his forehead. "I just, I don't know. I wasss ... not here... a forest?" He struggled to provide his friend with some explanation of his recent scattered visions.

Arka pointed ahead. "The woods are close, we've got to cross the cut first."

A loud hiss echoed about the chasm below, followed by a towering geyser rocketing into the sky. Ewan strained his eyes to see the bridge Arka was evidently intent on crossing extended out mere feet before it was engulfed by a veil of vapor.

"I ... uh ..." Ewan shook his head violently in attempts to hasten the indolent clearing of his thoughts and better express himself. Arka temporarily refrained from the crossing, perhaps realizing where his companion's mind had probably been.

"See yourself?" he questioned, as if simply asking for a lighter.

Ewan was still in too much disarray to respond by usual manner of aggressive agitation.

"I saw ... for myself?"

Arka seemed to expect such a reply, nodding in acceptance. A moment later, Ewan finally succeeded in shaking off his stupor. "What just happened? What'd I see?"

"More than likely, it was a residual effect of the brief moment you encountered yourself. I told you, shit seems to go ballistic. There's just no telling." Arka still received gestures of confusion from his friend.

"All right, look, think of it as replicating yourself every time you enter the dreamscape. I can't recall the total explanation for the life of me, but Atris buried himself in research on this stuff." Ewan sat down as another hiss sounded from over the edge. He looked up and prepared to digest the oncoming theory.

"Every visit to this world results in a projected copy, that either sways toward an adolescent variation or toward some point in adulthood – our early-thirties maybe."

Ewan laughed lowly at the concept of being thirty.

Arka continued.

"So, in theory, the result is two versions of the self, just on different points of the same timeline."

Ewan stood up and followed Arka onto the bridge. "So how you figure that's decided? Which way you go? The copy I mean."

"We don't really know, or at least I can't remember. I'd venture to guess that if you've gone through some sort of gain, whether educational or spiritual maybe, you'd mount on the side of the older rendition. Under opposite circumstances, you'd sway to the more inexperienced one."

"So that's why you called me 'the first time'? But it's possible I've been here before?"

"Possibly," Arka said. "I just don't know much about it. Again, it was really Atris's research. Conscious Fusion, he called it. ... Let's keep moving. The moons dropping."

Ewan glanced up at the shining disc, which was indeed no longer right above them, having initiated its descent to the horizon. He had paid it little attention through the march across the plains, though he figured it would now develop into prominent worry. He carefully continued after Arka, bringing his vision level with the bridge and bracing for another geyser as the hissing grew louder. Dislodged rocks fell from somewhere behind him. Ewan looked back, searching through the mist. Sure enough, the geyser erupted a few feet away, ensnaring the immediate steam and transporting the shroud skyward for a few short seconds.

Ewan saw something on the cliff, near where they had started on the bridge. He thought he could discern the shape of a man latched against the rock.

"We gotta keep going, 'fore things get worse," Arka beckoned from ahead. The canyon below moaned as the concealment of the fog returned and the pressure below commenced compounding.

"How can things get any worse than this?" Ewan jested as he reluctantly followed.

"You know that saying some asshole came up with at some point: Things could always be worse?" Arka's voice sounded from the mist, "I can't stress enough just how true that is."

★★★★

Nico continued through the thick forest in equal measure of carefree abandon and curiosity. The girl in white was all he could think about since he veered off the path and left Ewan. He tried focusing on something else.

He was not a man that displayed emotion needlessly, though he spoke his mind in a stout manner, always filtering through his doubts and qualms meticulously before vocalizing. This may have had something to do with his stature and strength. He was a fighter, the kind of guy that didn't put up with any form of laziness or needless excuses. His only downfall was his notoriously short temper that betrayed his otherwise razor-wit and high intelligence. Whatever the case, he didn't detect any prevailing urgency, even though he could barely remember anything prior the woods.

There was some matter of importance he was supposed to remember, some warning, but he couldn't recall what it might be. He came to a welcome clearing in the dense wood, a grassy hill that caught the breeze in waves. The earlier conversation with Ewan bred sufficient thought to merit some solitary evaluation and this seemed an ideal place for respite and retrospection. He made his way to the top of the shallow grade and sat amidst the soft, yellow grass, letting the wind caress his face and lull his eyelids down. A certain measure of self-control came over him.

He was suspicious Ewan might be harboring more than he divulged. Nico recalled they had seen some good times together to the point of becoming friends; well, beyond acquaintances at least. Nothing else came to light of their friendship, suffice to say Ewan consistently came off abrasive, and Nico didn't care much for being talked down to.

This had to be a dream, a particularly lucid one in truth, and he was determined to figure it out for himself rather than wasting energy gallivanting through the woods with the image of some bloke he went to school with. They might have been brothers at one point, but he got the notion that period had passed some time ago.

Part of the blame for such occurrences simply fell to age. Over time Nico's web of close friends had grown increasingly tight knit, and any expansion into the social scene ultimately required more cultivation than it was worth. A great deal of decent friends and relations had already faded into memory and stories, pictures and passing conversations.

It was as if maintaining old friendships somehow became too tasking as the years passed. In most cases, the remaining blame likely laid on repeated life lessons – the harsh kind, the kind that take a while to recover from. Arrests, deaths, overdoses, and other horrible anecdotes alike harden the hearts of many and cause some to resort inward. You inherently learn to keep to yourself more as you grow older anyway, out of self-defense. Take a wife, take a family and go from blood, right? That was a prospective route Nico was sure he wasn't ready to commit to anytime soon. What would be the point?

Ah, perhaps the wholesome pursuit of the American dream. He hesitated. What the hell was Americana anyway? Or what had it become? Was it just some fleeting notion with varying definitions, or was it simply fifties-era propaganda? A post-war set of suggestions on how people should go on living after losing damn near an entire generation beyond the islands of the Pacific or the shores of France. The steady job and standing in the small-town community, the happy wife, the jovial, successful children, the four-bedroom house? And the two-car garage? The white picket deal?

All of it sounded honest enough, though it had long since become outdated. Indeed, society has shifted tremendously in the past half-century. Nico shuddered at what prospective "American dream" might be adopted a couple decades down the line. He envisioned scantily clad girls everywhere, tricked-out cars with obnoxious sound systems getting five miles to the gallon, excessive gold jewelry, and rampant plastic surgery and boob-job clinics. The entire culture would be plugged into constant voluntary social surveillance, their smartphones grafted onto forearms, reflecting what rays of sun still penetrated the stratosphere through the smog.

Shit, enough of that. He could sit here all night pondering social order, but his attention was better spent contemplating his current predicament. In darkness, he reached back, as far as his short-term memory could afford him. When had he slept last? Was this a bad cut of fish? He sat there cross-legged and continued sifting through his memory. How did this all start?

"Chasing that first time – well it's never the same." Arka's voice was nostalgic as he brought a cigarette to his face.

"Bloody hell, I can't figure out what Atris was getting at here." Brac's figure came next, from left of Nico's field of vision. He was flipping through pages of a composition book. There was a thick haze all about them.

Arka exhaled. "Volume nine, that's the last one–"

"Someone's coming," Nico cut in. His words flowed naturally and without initiative. The sound of a rock skipping over concrete jumped up from down the road.

"Ah, another wanderer of the night," Arka observed, unthreatened.

"Maybe the fellow's an illusion," Brac excitedly proposed in a low voice. The approaching figure raised his hood, coming up on the position of their circle.

"Yeah, but it hasn't even started yet." Ewan emerged from the tree line to respond to Brac's proposal.

"It's takin' forever." Nico's voice sounded as the unknown traveler passed. An ominous breeze cut through the night.

"No. ... It's already started." Arka's words now betrayed his earlier abandon.

Brac was tracking the figure that had passed. "Was that – am I really seeing shit?"

"Well," Arka nodded. "I didn't think we'd be at this level so soon."

"About time," Nico said eagerly, stretching out his shoulders.

Brac closed the notebook and sheathed his pen at his side. "Shall we then?"

Ewan remained quiet, surveying the asphalt expanse that had produced the stranger.

Nico stepped beside him. They had come to this back-road maze in the middle of the night, another weekend's poised problem of boredom with no solutions. Some type of ruined structure was supposed to be nearby, an old forest-fire watchtower that had since fallen into disuse. They must've been out there looking for it, but now strangeness was taking hold. They had placed their bets and the night was posed to play its hand. Arka and Brac's conversation became undiscernible. Nico looked at Ewan to see his uneasy smile fade.

"We got lights!" he said, whirling around to the others. The wind surged without warning, and the streetlight above them flickered once and ceased. Arka smote his cigarette underfoot, noticing what first appeared to be headlights had now tripled in number and weren't restricted to the street.

"Let's move."

The boys made a break for a nearby church, Arka and Brac heading up the small column in flight. Nico found himself running, trying to keep pace. Cardio truly proved his physical weak point, and he opted to veer off into a neighboring side yard. Ewan flew by his position as the lights closed in.

"In here!"

Nico swallowed his skipped heartbeat resulting from the feminine voice sounding not six feet away. He could see the slim figure of a girl peering from behind the door of a large shed. He got up from his crouched position as the forest around him lit up like a rave. This wasn't the cops; this was something else. He dove into the shed, and the girl quietly shut the door behind them.

"Thanks," Nico said between shallow breaths. "Don't mean to scare you. My friends and I were just—"

He was alone. In fact, it was quite possibly the emptiest shed in existence. Two windows permitted the growing light entry as it filled the small room. He stood up, mounting courage to exit and face whatever craziness had come out of nowhere. The door flew open and he was overtaken by blinding light.

Nico opened his eyes and breathed heavily, falling back onto the soft grass of the hill. So Ewan had been there at the start of this ordeal. The girl in white had been there as well. Her image was all too enticing.

"Hope I see her again."

"Good evening to you!" A soft voice sang out from the tree line, carried on the faintest of warm breezes. Nico jumped up and turned to see her coming up the hill. He wasn't as stunned as he anticipated he would've been. The girl walked over to his position, barely disturbing the ground, breaking not a single twig beneath her feet. She was of fit build and stood substantially shorter than Nico, with red hair swaying about her shoulders in waves. Her skin was fair and her smile was flawless. "Hey there."

Nico smiled. "You're in this too. ... Figure you might know what's going on here – if you don't mind?"

She let out a small laugh. "I wish I knew."

"It was you – at the shed earlier," Nico continued. "What were those lights?"

The girl looked to the sky. "The lights brought us all here."

"Then you've seen the others?"

"I have. We are all headed to the same place." She pointed down the far path. "North."

Nico embodied confidence, "Right, well, mind if I travel with you?"

"Not at all," she started, bringing her hands up to her face suddenly. "Oh, I'm sorry. My name is Aislin." She held out her hand, letting her diaphanous garb fall back to her sides.

"Nico. Nice to meet you." They shook hands and started off down the path, heading north, as far as Aislin's directions were sound. In truth, Nico didn't really care where they were going. The growl of thunder echoed from the far west.

8

Someone sought our static
the seekers prayed for havoc
and the toll pried deep within the dust of time.
Blind maidens sing songs of retrograde amnesia
and the sirens sleep forever under constant anesthesia
And now we're folding back,
on the separate sails of the gales that never saw the light of land
vexed between the might of the mind and the tests of the hand.
And now we're reeling under attack,
The razor eyes did subdivide and write themselves a fickle end.

Lightning stabbed the cliff face to the right, shattering boulders and ejecting shards of rock into the air. Atris looked on in disbelief as the stone shower careened into the river with thunderous splashes that were still dwarfed by the howling wind. He still held the severed towline. Their raft was now powerless, at the mercy of the storm, and they were heading dangerously close to the electricity-eliciting cliffs.

"Come on!" Brac yelled. He and Arka were busy fashioning a crude rigging of sail from their shirts and hoodies, the driving rain stinging their bare shoulders as they gripped the deck rings with one hand and strained to harness the power of the tempest. Atris followed suit and lashed out for the center point of the rigging. Arka leaned back as far as he could manage, hanging over toward port stern to compensate for the rightward track.

"It's one damn disaster after another here!" Atris vigorously fought to affix the billowing clothesline under the leading-edge logs. The three misfit mariners peered through the driving rain to witness distance grow between them and the cliffs. Fortunately, the wind was surging upstream through the bottleneck. The boys continued to adjust for the river's center.

Brac was laughing wildly. "It's working!"

★★★★

Ewan was sure his guide was merely a few feet ahead of him on the bridge, but he couldn't see a thing in the rising steam. The only indications Arka was even there was the occasional jerk on the rope handrails or whistle prompting Ewan's haste. It was getting hotter and he was worried they'd soon begin to roast.

"It's all in the mind," he kept telling himself. "Nothing we can't handle." Another hiss compounded as pressure mounted at his six. The roar of the ensuing geyser was suddenly coupled with a loud crack from behind and the wooden planks instantly angled downward in response, the degree rising exponentially as Ewan's feet left the structure and he was launched into the air.

"Shit!" he shouted through the whirling steam, coming to a lull mid-air before beginning his descent into the chasm. He saw but a few feet in front of him until the planks instantly appeared before his face. He reached out, fiercely clawing for hold, catching a gap in the boards and riding the swing as it headed for the far cliff wall. Seconds later, the broken bridge smashed into the rocky ridge and the wood shattered in Ewan's hands. He flailed left and caught the side rope, gasping heavily to regain some composure.

"Ewan!" Arka called from above. "Hold on!"

Ewan planted his feet against the rock and wrapped the line about his knuckles. Step by step, he toiled vertically, the rope in his grasp pulling him up at a steady clip. He looked down at the swirling mass of illuminating steam, and he could swear he saw arms outstretch from the shroud, mere meters beneath his feet.

He focused, tensed his arms and back, and balanced his legs to continue his ascent. Another hiss began to rise.

"Come on!" Arka shouted through strain.

Ewan reeled, hand-over-hand until his feet left the cliff and he went sprawling to the soft ground left in its absence. The rope slackened, and Arka ran to his side.

"Something's," Ewan spoke between heaves for breath, "Something's down, there."

"What?"

Ewan sat up to brush himself off as another geyser erupted from the chasm. He heaved through gritted teeth. "Before we go any further, what's happening here?"

Arka helped his friend to his feet and readied some rugged rendition of an explanation. "Basically, this place is falling apart. The steam is coming from the borders of the world beneath."

Ewan winced at the terminology as Arka continued.

"I don't know why it's happening, but I'd guess it's a sign that the proverbial hourglass is truly running low. Are you all right?"

"All right? I'm awesome," Ewan snapped. "You know it's not every day you go through close calls like that, and you just don't know how you'll perform until your muscles prime and tenacity takes over. Instinct, man, and explosive adrenaline." He shouted wildly and kicked a stone back into the chasm.

"Right then," Arka said. "Swiftly through the forest now." He made his way down the path to the entrance of the dense wood beyond.

Ewan followed. "I almost feel like I've been here before."

"Definitely not coming back though, eh?" Arka joked. "It'd be like…" Arka's words became muffled and indiscernible, as a voice belonging to neither of them entered Ewan's mind.

"But you still better come back for us!" It rose and fell in volume, echoing momentarily, before fading to nothing.

"Ewan!" Arka shouted, shocking him back to the task before them. "What is it?"

Ewan shook his head wildly, "I just–" he paused. "Someone fell?" It was as if he posed the question to himself, the shape of a hand outstretching into his mind.

"Well, you just did, but you're fine now. Come on, forget it," Arka demanded. Ewan obliged, and the two proceeded into the wall of trees before them.

★★★★

Atris's boots splashed down into the shallows, midway up to his shins. Arka disembarked the battered raft and helped Brac fumble with the network of knots to free their clothes rendered rags. They soon made their way ashore, trudging after Atris to a beach with sand as black as cinder.

Brac came to stand on Atris's right, gazing up at a magnificent waterfall some hundred yards away. Arka fell next to them and rolled over, still heaving in spite of the battle upstream. They sized up matters within the enveloping shadow of the mountain range before them. It spanned the blackened shore and loomed into the sky above.

"Great, more rain," Brac observed as something lightly fell to his forehead. He wiped it off, his knuckle leaving a black smear on his brow.

"It's ash." Atris lowered his sight to the ground as he finally caught his breath.

"I don't like this," Arka stated the obvious shared viewpoint as they continued studying the obstructed sky.

"The moon," Atris said. "It's already about to fall behind that peak there. We've got to move."

"What's the rush?" Arka asked, simply enjoying his newfound state of dryness and stability.

"I don't know." Atris pushed off the ground and immediately headed in the direction of the waterfall. "Call it a hunch. … I've just got a rising bad feeling something big is about to happen."

"Something big? The hell was all that then?!" Brac angrily inquired.

Arka said nothing as he followed Brac and Atris toward the intimidating cliff.

Moments later, they reached the crashing cascade of water and what proved to be quite the formidable climb ahead of them. Atris started feeling out cutaways and footholds.

"Maybe we should try to find a way around," Arka suggested. "That's got to be a good eighty feet to the top."

"Don't be a bitch," Brac voiced his support of Atris's proposed path.

"There are already footholds, dude. And it's not like it's straight up." Atris began to ascend the rock wall in deft fashion, Brac eagerly at his heels.

In truth, Arka noticed no alternative route upon scanning their surroundings. In the dim fashion of an oncoming dawn, he could discern little detail or distinct features in the coastline. The mountains came right down to the ashen beaches, providing no other way forward within the small domain of the newfound cove.

Resigned, he joined the others as they steadily climbed, a short distance to the right of the raging waterfall. Arka had underestimated the elevation, but was reassured by the speed at which his two companions moved up the slope ahead of him. He looked back in the direction of the river, to see the gargantuan thunderhead making its way west.

"Hope we don't run into another one of those," Brac said from a few feet above.

Arka continued scanning the horizon. "It's strange. One thing after another in this place. We made it ashore, but I still feel like we're adrift on a merciless sea."

"The tides of time," Brac submitted.

Atris grunted from above. "Sure makes you feel alive."

Brac laughed. "If the ups and downs of my life were this close together, things would certainly be a lot more interesting."

"Well let's put this up behind us before something else happens," Arka recommended.

They continued their ascent and, within minutes, Arka was pulling himself up to roll over the edge onto level ground.

He sat up to see the massive circular lake that fed the mighty fall. There were a small number of peaks protruding into the horizon, few of which were much higher than their current position. The limited light granted from the sky revealed a field of scattered craters, with the lake itself seemingly formed as a result of some high-impact projectile. Arka noticed a spire silhouetted off in the distance, bathed in the backlight of the low moon.

"We should make for the tower there." Atris cast his hand to the north.

"Why?" Arka asked coldly.

"Well for one, there's light over there. And for some reason I feel it's where we should go." Atris turned and folded his arms. "Got a better idea?"

Arka looked to Brac for his vote, but Brac only sighed and followed Atris as he started off around the lake. The steady rain of ash continued falling lightly from above as Arka fell in line behind the others, ultimately always trusting the gut of his long-standing brother.

"Don't get me wrong," Atris was saying as he caught up. "We just don't really have anything else to go on right now. We haven't seen anyone else besides you, and who knows where the others might be?"

"There might not even be anyone else in this place," Brac responded. "Dreams don't count for any rules. You know this."

"You really still think we're dealing with a common dream here?" Arka asked.

Atris stopped. "Common? No, but–"

"Look!" Brac cut him off and took off running. Atris and Arka paused their debate and focused on what lay ahead. Ash was no longer the sole occupant of the immediate sky above. Scattered embers floated down in majestic fashion, illuminating the barren cinder stretch before them.

Brac came to wait at an old stone wall forged of perhaps pumice or some other white rock, precariously placed in the middle of the black field.

"Get a loada that," Arka said, reaching the wall and glaring at the flurry of fire ahead. The ground shook slightly.

"Arka!"

He whirled around to his friends, who were still sizing up the foreboding sight ahead. The voice didn't belong to them, though it still seemed somewhat familiar.

"Did you say something?" he asked.

"No," Brac said, Atris shaking his head in turn. Arka scanned the area in the manner of a mother who lost her child in a metro station.

"I thought I just heard…"

★★★★

"Arka! Bro!" Ewan's voice slipped back into prevalence once more. "Dude, you been fadin' on me again. I told you, there's like a treehouse up ahead." Arka shook himself out of his daze. He and Ewan had made steady progress through the forest, short his own guidance, which he originally believed to be superior to that of his comrade. On contrary, since they first entered the dense wood, it was Ewan who had flawlessly sought out which paths to take, claiming he recalled having been there before. Arka felt he should be the one to retain level head and solid bearings, though he was instead being shown up and out-focused by a first time.

What had he just seen though? Torches? No matter.

"Compose yourself," he muttered under his breath.

"Hey!" Ewan shouted once again. "You listenin'? There's a door over here! So does that mean one of us put it there at some point? … Aren't you supposed to know these things?"

"Not necessarily." Arka adjusted his hoodie and fumbled around his pockets, searching for a cigarette that again proved absent.

He caught up with Ewan, who was standing before a large pine door set into the side of a massive fallen redwood. The mammoth trunk boasted all kinds of moss, fungi, and beautiful flowers throughout, only now admirable in the light of impending daybreak.

"Isn't it amazing?" Arka asked in reverence. "In nature, how death gives way to countless occurrences of life? All abundant variations, all from just one grand instance of death. … Humans gotta be the only species on the planet that don't traditionally give back after we die. We box ourselves up in the ground or reduce ourselves to ash in an urn instead."

Ewan eyed him, his disregard for such philosophical observations written on his face. Arka knew his friend considered such matters pointless to think on. To him, death was death and it was just as simple as that. It's finite. It's the end. He had once claimed being dead would bother him just about as much as the time before he was born bothered him. Ewan moved up to further inspect the door, leaving Arka to continue his survey.

Arka sighed and glanced down the fallen giant spanning into the black of the forest, taking in their total surroundings beyond the immediate splendor of the natural garden. He realized the trunk came to rest against a rocky incline that gradually steepened into the failing dark.

"We must've reached the north end of the woods," he said.

A twig snapped from somewhere in the dense forest.

★★★★

"That's good, right?" Ewan questioned, suspiciously surveying the trees. He let impatience play his hand instead of waiting for an answer. All he had to do was lean on the door, and it effortlessly swung open, creaking on its hinges. A faint light played on the tunnel inside, spilling onto the ground before him. Subtle rises and falls in the orange glow could be seen, sure characteristics of some flame emitting from around the corner.

To his surprise, Arka entered the cave immediately, without a word. Ewan followed him into a large chamber, well lit by flames dancing inside metal lanterns clinging to the walls, crowned with laurel designs. Flowers and vines weaved a web of flora about the room's every surface, with a brick fireplace on the far side housing a hypnotic blaze. Arka made his way over to it and sat down, warming his hands while Ewan continued to scan the cavernous room.

There seemed to be a network of tunnels in an upper level, reached via an ascending staircase cut into the wall on the right, with a contrasting staircase in the wall to their left descending below. The walls were a soft, reddish hue carved of the very mountainside, adorned with a variety of artwork peeking out between the stretching embrace of the vines, garlanded in all manner of orchids, lilies, carnations, and roses. While botany was one of Arka's key interests, Ewan felt his lack of such knowledge proved a benefit in the inspiring display around him.

It was in the same manner he didn't want to know the scientific explanation for why the sky was blue; or precisely what accounted for the sunset throwing all multitudes of reds and yellows about the stratosphere. Why he wouldn't watch any of the special features and exploitive content of his favorite movies. Or similarly, why music videos set to his favorite songs were blacklisted. Sometimes becoming aware of why or how things happen takes away from the beauty of it all. The overall magic you get through your own unadulterated perspective dwindles under explanations.

"I expected some of you would find me."

Ewan and Arka jumped up, backing against each other. They failed to discern the source of the small bout of laughter that followed the carefree voice harmoniously ricocheting off the stone walls. Though there was no threat in the female's tone —quite the opposite rather — neither of the boys were in the mood for surprises or trickery this late in the game.

"No reason to be so jumpy." The sound of gentle footsteps came from the stairs in the right wall.

"Who's there?" Ewan's question was aggressive, and Arka shot his elbow back, jabbing him in his right kidney. Ewan hunched over in shock. He was considering retaliation against the cheap shot, but his concentration was cut upon seeing the girl that had just entered the room.

She was dressed in an olive-green skirt of a leafy tessellation that fit snug around her waist, hanging down about her knees. Her midsection was barely visible from underneath a tight shirt of deep earthen tones and soft jade linings, and her shoulders were covered only by her flowing golden hair.

She was stunning for sure, but Ewan resumed contemplating a counterattack against Arka, releasing pressure on his tender side and rising to his feet.

"Right, well?" he asked, defensively facing his friend while questioning the girl.

She motioned toward a stretch of moss near the fireplace. "Won't you sit and stay? At least for a drink?"

Ewan clenched his fists and looked to Arka. "Okay, that's your cue. Gotta keep moving this, running out of time that — north, books, tower and moon and shit." His taunting fell on deaf ears.

Arka eyed the girl. "I've — seen you before." He followed her over to the moss and sat beside her, leaning back on his elbows. She was looking quite carelessly into the fire, a perfect smile of white catching the light of the flames.

"You have." Her voice was warm. "It must've been a long time ago, Arka." She placed her hand on top of his. "But I recognize you. How thankful I am that you found me. I figured the whole lot of you would pass me by."

Ewan was suddenly worried, fishing for an idea as to exactly why. He couldn't produce any evidence to validate his escalating unease. Perhaps it was simply because night was fading, and he knew they had to get to their destination by morning. He figured Arka was too intrigued to yield to caution, and his frame yearned for rest, though sitting around here had to be a decisive waste of time; drink or no drink, vixen or not. Why wasn't Arka realizing the same?

He continued struggling to remember the girl. Had she come there with them? Or maybe she's one of those writers marooned here; a victim of a fate Arka said might befall them if they didn't hurry. Ewan couldn't hear what they were saying now, their conversation drowned out by the soft growl of the fire, the racing of his cluttered worries, or some other nervous force at work.

"Hey! Listen lady, love to stay in your pretty cave here, but we need to get to the archives ASAP," he interjected, derailing whatever pleasant exchange they were having. They both turned over their shoulders to see him.

"The library?" She asked in turn.

"Yeah, with, uh, the tower." Ewan was pleased to gain some sort of following.

"It's right down that way." She smiled again and motioned to the descending stair. "I write there so often, I have my own way in." She paused. "I stay out here to be around the wonders of life within this world. Halls of stone get so musty and dreary over time, colorless even. The energy is all there, though the splendor is trapped within text, caged in the canvas of the reader's intangible imagination." She was almost swaying as she spoke, as if reciting a cherished poem.

"Here, only out here, magic is all around you. It floats, you breathe it in, your eyes flutter through radiance, and your ears bear witness to the soft symphonies of the forest, instead of the empty echoes of a marble hall." Her tone shifted slightly in the latter part of her musing, heavy a hint of melancholy.

"Still too many limitations out here. An emptiness in solace, for we can have all the treasure of the earth, but its worth is moot without someone else present to share in the beauty." Ewan thought to inquire as to what she was getting at, but the girl continued on. "So many works there my own, in truth. Keeping them among the rest just feels right and helps me remember in times of doubt."

"Right, well there you have it, down that way," Ewan said hastily, dismissing fledgling curiosity. He was fairly certain she wasn't one of theirs and she was clearly getting by swimmingly in her mountain-hole here. "Arka, let's get a move on, man. That-a-way."

"Relax brother. …Chill for a few minutes. We've been traveling all night and there's a heavy climb ahead. Mary's a friend. She's got a gallery up there she wants us to check out, her own works and what." Ewan quelled Arka's rising veneration with an angry stare. "And maybe it will spell something out for us, help us figure out what we're up against."

Arka didn't otherwise come off worried at all, turning back to admire the fire. Ewan clenched his fists again, angered by his comrade's apathy regarding what had been their most dire of goals until recently. He watched on, as this Mary leaned over to whisper something into Arka's ear.

"I'm going, bro." Ewan made his way to the stairs. "And you need to come with me. Don't know what I'm getting into up ahead. We need to stick together. Can't be much time left."

"Time?" Mary said softly. "Oh, there's no need to be worrying about that, Ewan. Time doesn't matter down here. You boys left it far behind when you arrived. All that matters now is what we feel, what we can create."

"Yeah, but we've got to get home," Ewan argued.

"Home?" Mary smiled wryly. "Do you even know what that is anymore? Has it not shifted and changed as your years have turned?" She continued on before Ewan could answer.

"You know it's not just where you wake up in the morning or where you store your possessions. It's not just a physical place, like it was when we were kids. Home has become a comprehension, a state of mind. And when we are no longer satisfied with our homes, we adapt, we find new ones."

Ewan was unmoved, "Speaking of waking—"

"We tried to wake up for so long," Mary interrupted yet again. "It really is irrelevant." An undertone of sadness crept into her voice. "Why would you want to?" she asked, in the lighthearted manner of a suggestion regarding lunch. Arka moved from his previous preoccupation of admiring the paintings on display to listen intently to her proclamations.

"We don't need to rejoin the blinded masses." She slowly raised her arms up, letting her head gently fall back to allow observation of the brilliant chandelier hanging from the ceiling's center point.

Ewan hadn't noticed its exquisiteness and intricacy before, dismissing a bunch of crystals on strings as no big deal. The preceding hand gesture had given him another chill. This chick was coming off a screwy daytime-television preacher.

"We don't need to go back, to conform to the frivolous habits of society," her sermon continued. "No matter how you size it all, life in the modern world is all ever about one thing: money. That's all they ever want there. Countless people sacrifice the best parts of their soul, their creativity and their innocence, in the pursuit of wealth, in security for fears. If ever a truer statement existed, it's that money is indeed the root of evil."

"Yeah, a necessary evil, maybe—" Ewan stopped himself short, having witnessed a thousand debates and disputes bridging the wide scope of these subjects. Atris and Arka always called it 'intelligent conversation'; he always opted the term 'bullshit'. He wouldn't play into her wild banter now.

Though Mary still went on, as if she was selling a notion to Arka.

"You won't grow old and bitter here. Love is all around you, abundant and priceless. You can retrieve your lost innocence. We can be reimbursed the cost of life's harshest lessons – those learned while we flailed for position in a society driving itself mad. There are no such corruptions here."

Ewan was growing increasingly nervous the more this girl's rant seemed to strengthen her grip on his friend. He'd heard Arka complain about these very things in the past – troubles with society, shortcomings of their culture and all that. Ewan had written them off in turn, just as he would disregard Atris's weightless theories. Mary spoke flowingly to Arka, her words coming off to Ewan in poison fashion of Homer's sirens of old.

"In truth, I wanted to go back just to have someone to talk to, someone to share my love with, to create with me." Mary smiled and fell back on her elbows to mirror Arka's posture. "You won't grow old and bitter here."

Ewan drew closer to them. He'd noticed Mary's repetition, though he seemed to be the only one perturbed by it. He expected her to echo something else she had already thrown out there, thus granting solid ground to grab his friend and make a dash for the exit; though she didn't deliver so.

"No more of the hard banalities integral our old social structure. No more paying the rising dues of an overly cautious and analytical nature fashioned out of adaptation through age. No risk of the sure loss that is to follow, given enough time. No more innocence for experience as a means to get through the years." Mary reached out and ran her slender fingers through Arka's hair. "We can be wanderlust caretakers of the life force, architects of paradise, feral children of the mind." She leaned in close.

"That's it!" Ewan's wavering patience dissolved. "Lady, you're insane."

Arka turned back with a flare in his eyes, though strangely did nothing to counter the offense.

"Sorry, Mary. It's been real, but time for us to go." Ewan stretched out his hand to help Arka to his feet.

"Time?" Mary questioned again, wielding a stern tone. "Time doesn't exist down here. All that matters now…" Her words faded.

Ewan braced himself and utilized his superior mass, gripping Arka's palm tightly before heaving him to his feet and toward the stairs in one full motion, his head suffering considerable impact against the wall.

Mary sat, silent and unmoving, staring back at Ewan with a very different, rancorous expression on her snow-white complexion. He couldn't look away from her, and the room vibrated. His vision blurred and his peripherals were obstructed by a shifting static of color. Sound was lost, save the steady drum of a beating heart. The only thing clear was Mary's gaze, crippling and unblinking. The ground shook violently, and it felt like it was about to split beneath his feet.

★★★★

"Did you feel that!?" Brac asked. He, Atris, and Arka had already traversed a good stretch across the expanse of the cinder plain.

"Earthquake!" Atris shouted, holding his arms out in front of him as if intending to stabilize the ground himself. Arka was vigorously massaging his temples in hopes of diminishing a sharp pain that had recently filled his head. All of the sudden, the rumbling beneath them came to a surge and the mountain bordering the left of the plain produced a thunderous roar.

"Not good!" Atris shouted, glaring at the groaning giant with Arka at his side.

"Hell with this!" Brac was made a blur as he leapt into full sprint and passed his fellow travelers where they stood, trying his best to run over ground that was continually failing at its job.

"Well, you heard the man!" Arka followed their fleeing friend as a loud crack cut through the night and resounded off the farthest of peaks. The summit to their left was gone, and in its place was now a great plume of ash rocketing into the heavens, drawing out an ever-increasing envelope of orange and red. Molten death collected at the point of rupture and began to overflow, spilling down the mountainside.

"Here they come!" Atris shouted as he passed Arka in stride. Brac was still ahead, running diligently and watching the skies as the impending firestorm leered down on them. Scattered boulders and massive chunks of rock cut through the black night, leaving vibrant orange trails in their wake as they fell about the Runners. They peppered the ash-laden field, blasting up fountains of gravel and debris in vicious volleys. Arka fought wildly for breath, attempting to gain on Atris and Brac. He caught a flare out of the corner of his eye, and was suddenly launched through the air. He hit the ground rolling and scrambled for footing.

Listen again to the wind as it hits your heart
decipher the message, turn 'round the tragedy
absorb a new form of sanctuary
more profound than us
staring into the atlas, staring into time
more profound than yours
more profound than mine

Arka struggled to his feet in a disorientated stupor. Mary was unmoving, fixated, looking into Ewan. The ground continued to shake ferociously beneath them, and Arka worried the cave might not hold. The ornate chandelier was beginning to break free from its suspension. He felt his muscles fighting for the simplest of movements, but in the next second he was shocked free from paralysis by another new voice. It resonated through every inch of the cave, overcoming the steady rumble in a booming echo.

"We tried to wake up for so long. But you know that can't happen. Like you said, it really is irrelevant."

Though he could not see him, Arka knew who spoke.

"Greer!" he shouted up toward the cave's ceiling. "Where are you?!"

"No way dude, no way," Ewan said frantically. "Let's get out of here!"

Arka glanced over to see Mary on her feet, apparently terrified.

"You leave us alone!" she shouted to the cave's ceiling. "Don't you come in here to taunt me!"

"There's not much time left, brothers." Greer's voice resounded through the cave once more in warning.

"Arka! We're leaving, now!" Ewan sprinted for the stairs, only to be beaten to the threshold by Mary, who held her arms out in barricade fashion, sporting the feverish stare of a devout goalkeeper.

"There's still time," Arka said, coming up beside Ewan and sending him from a state of panic to rage.

Ewan geared up for a trademark tirade. "I'll bet you anything we been in here so long talking to this broad that the sun's out and we're screwed! That's what you said would happen, right? Are we gonna end up like her?!"

Arka studied Mary, only now noticing an accessory of some notability. The dull silver chain she wore around her neck sustained a small pendant that must've escaped the confines of her shirt during her dash for the tunnel. The charm was an arrangement of leaf-shaped, ruby-red stones, fanning out in succession as if the tail feathers of a shining red cardinal. Arka had seen it before, for it had long since been affixed to the bulletin board above Atris's desk.

"But, how is it–?" Arka started, silencing Ewan's rant.

Mary must have sensed his change in demeanor, or the passing realization; whatever the case, her eyes betrayed her confidence.

"What are you doing here, Juli?" Arka asked.

"...I knew I had seen—" Ewan recoiled, taking two steps back from a now trembling Mary. "What's she doing here?" He hesitantly repeated Arka's inquiry.

"It's been how many years? Heard you were on the run." Arka attempted to evaluate Mary's reaction, but she would no longer look his way. The cave jolted violently and the chandelier came down just a few feet behind them, in a shockwave of shattering crystal.

"That's it!" Ewan charged through Mary's defense and took off down the stairs.

Arka was in a certain state of awe that somehow took precedence over fear of entombment. "We heard you were – I mean you were lost when you left but – how is it you're in this place?"

His only response from the girl was a short whimper. Mary lowered her arms and fell to her knees.

"We—" Arka faltered. "We never heard from you, only what rumors went around."

The shaking candle-lit lanterns flickered wildly as if a great gale tore through the cavern.

"Come with us, Juli." Arka offered out his hand.

Mary shamefully withdrew and her arms descended to her waist. Arka sighed, the quake intensifying all around them.

"This place is going to go!" Ewan's voice came from far-off down the tunnel, barely discernable amidst the rolling din.

Mary recoiled, springing to her feet and pressing her back to the wall. "You don't need to go back. There is nothing for you at the end of that road!" Her sadness shifted to aggressive persistence once more.

Arka looked at the floor and then down the passageway. In the wake of his wild dash downward, he left Mary standing there, her eyes fading to the solid white of pearls.

She shrieked. Her words bounced wildly off the walls, making light work of drowning out the roar around them. "You'll still come back for us!"

Arka charged forward and up a steep incline toward a dim light ahead. He glanced over his shoulder, only to see the ceiling give in behind him, rubble crashing down and speeding a wall of orange dust to his heels.

Mary's last words seemed to echo on much longer than they should have.

★★★★

"Come back for us!" Arka found himself shouting as the fire continued to fall around him in full amateur-shooting-gallery fashion.

Atris was upon him in a second, instantaneously flinging him to his feet and back into maximum pace. They'd covered a great expanse from the white wall, but the lava flow had made its way down the mountainside to begin its rampage across the field, consuming the dull black with fierce, brilliant orange.

Brac slackened his pace, coming up alongside them. "We're not going to make it!" It was hard enough to maintain footing with the ground moving so violently and there was still substantial distance to cover before they reached the scattered peaks of the plain's far side.

They felt the intensity of the furious flow creeping up on them when another jarring crack sounded through the sky. The mountain bordering the field on its right split straight down its center. In the following seconds, a large gash bounded through the black terrain in the same manner of a failing frozen lake spidering beneath their weight. It resembled a negative image of the forked lightning that recently appeared in the northern sky, ripping its way through the rock as if it were a field of tall corn at the mercy of the sharpest of scythes.

"Well, that's that," Arka said, dejectedly slowing from sprint to a low jog. The fissure was heading straight for them. He fell to one knee with his head down, desperately trying to regain his breath, feeling the intense heat of the lava flow rapidly approaching from his left. This might not be so bad. They'd probably just wake up.

"Keep running!" Brac yelled from somewhere up ahead.

As quickly as it had come into being, the gaping newborn chasm was upon them and shot directly across their path, viciously spitting gravel into the air. Arka looked up to see Atris launch himself high off the shaking ground; Brac had already disappeared into the curtain of dust.

"Yes," Arka managed to get out through the heavy rhythm of his breathing. "Reckon I need to see where this madness goes." He took what few seconds were left to recall the indisputable lucidity of his journey so far, and realized he hadn't told himself this all had to be a dream for quite some time. He still couldn't remember how it all happened, how they got there, or if there was a point to any of this.

He sighed heavily, having no inclination as to why he was out of breath in a dream, why he could see every detail of every shaking pebble beneath his tired feet, or why he could physically feel the compounding heat at his flank.

The dust born of the newfound gash had settled; the molten tide at Arka's heels. He could barely make out Atris and Brac shouting wildly in the distance, their features becoming more discernible in the growing orange light. From a three-point stance he leapt forth, shot from his gravel footing, traces of lava seeping into the small indentations left behind.

Arka flew through wild strides toward his friends, reaching the fresh edge and leaping through the air, arms outstretched. He fell just short of the far plain and slammed into the cliff wall, heart sinking as he braced for the imminent plummet to God knows what.

He felt contact on his arms and clenched his hands tight, looking up to see Brac and Atris leaning over to his aid. He tightened every muscle in his upper body and his comrades pulled him up. They all followed through leverage to land safely, their backs against the vibrating gravel. The lava overtook the fissure, slowly spilling downwards in a vivid cascade. The ground beneath them settled, the quake fast subsiding to nothing, leaving only the sound of scorching rock and the low groan of the churning molten flow.

"Ha ha HAH!" Brac laughed maniacally and jumped to his feet, throwing his arms into the air. Atris rose and stepped to the cliff's edge, admiring the fiery torrent. Only Arka remained on the ground, staring at the sky above as he tried to calm himself after nearly being incinerated.

"Get a look at that," Atris said calmly, as if they were never in any danger at all. "It's amazing – how such might, such unstoppable devastation can be so beautiful, almost tranquil."

Brac was still laughing lowly.

Arka stood up and brushed himself off, moving to his friend's side and crossing his arms in distaste. "Yeah, real pretty. Let's get out of here before that fills up or something else blows up."

Brac suppressed his twisted bliss and pointed northward again, "The tower seems pretty close." Another branching flash of lightning faded in and out of view as the boys scanned the northern sky. They continued on at a stiff pace across what remained of the black plain. Arka followed closely behind the others. He was still doing his best to regain his composure, analyzing every step of what had just happened. Why were his words so unfounded before? Where had they come from? If that chasm hadn't split at that very minute, they all would have—

His prevailing modus of dismissing unanswerable worries and frightening illusions to be simply spins of a dream was proving evermore ineffective. He was finally convinced something far more profound was at work.

★★★★

"Well, THAT was messed up!" Ewan shouted as his friend finally caught up to him. The tunnel had stopped shaking, and he figured they were safe for now. The light of what appeared to be an exit could be seen just up ahead.

"Uh, yeah. Poor girl." Arka rubbed the side of his head.

Ewan scoffed, "I knew something was up with that chick man. But no, you were all, there's no rush, let's just stay here for a bit, she's a friend man."

"Juli *was* a friend. You remember her."

Ewan shrugged. "Yeah, I recognized her, but we haven't seen or heard from her in years. So she's just some crazy production of this nightmare world, some fragment of a girl we remember. That's not the real Juli."

Arka leaned against the cave wall. "Yeah, it doesn't make sense – as if much does in this place. I remember Atris trying to reach her for a couple years, after she moved to far away wherever." Arka hesitated. "And when we find Atris, don't tell 'em about her."

Ewan wasn't too concerned. "You really think there is some purpose for seeing her here?"

"I don't know," Arka said. "It's just … I felt her back there. I don't think it was a manifestation stemming from our collective psyche. And I figured Greer's involvement in all of this was just him helping me through it. But those words were clear and you heard him too."

Ewan didn't answer and instead moved on to the exit.

"Something else is going on here, Ewan. Something far more serious than—"

Ewan whirled around just before reaching the tunnel's end. "Would you shut the hell up and just worry about getting outta here? There is definitely no time left to stand around some mineshaft discussing ghosts of the Run!" Ewan sensed he might finally be getting through to Arka, as he silently made his way over.

"You know," he started up again, "for apparently being the more learned one of us, you sure like to take your chances in this place. And you keep telling me there's more time, when you really can't know how much we have left. Or were you just after some tail back there? You don't remember shit." Ewan stopped flailing his arms and clenched his fists, readying defense against another possible kidney shot as Arka approached his position, though he seemed to no longer be paying mind to Ewan's accusations. The lit area ahead took form.

"What did you say?" Arka asked calmly.

Ewan scoffed. "Whatever, man."

"No, really. What'd you say? The bit about time."

"We don't have any left. Let's go!" Ewan set foot off the red dirt and onto pearl-white marble.

"Of course." Arka said clearly. "The rules – have to heed the rules. You're right, man."

"What?" Ewan stared off into the chamber.

"The fourth rule," Arka said, stepping into the light.

They stood in a magnificent room of marble and granite. Massive Romanesque columns stretched high to a ceiling supporting multitudes of flickering candles. Elegant laurels and spiraled designs of Celtic influence bordered deep chestnut walls boasting an array of overburdened bookshelves forged of oak. There were ascending marble staircases to either side, leading to an upper level that stretched much further than they could discern from below. Contrastingly, a recess in the floor twenty feet from where they stood gave way to a descending spiral staircase of glass.

"We're here." Arka folded his arms. "And there's still time."

Rule Number Four: Always have time.

Own it. Shape it yours. This doesn't have to be achieved through maintaining a schedule or drafting an itinerary, just always remember it exists. Utilize it to pull yourself out of despair and the very deepest of inward introspections, when your mind may be stuck in a loop or you become fixated on grave matters and unreal things that don't exist by any account of duration. Know the prospect of moving forward with your life is a beautiful one indeed, and even though you might be stuck for a spell, you'll get back at it again. Know you are part of a world that runs on the man-made device of time, and that, when viewed correctly, it will indeed heal all, as they say.

★★★★

"You say something?" Brac looked back inquisitively.

"—just," Arka said. "Time heals all."

Brac smiled. "Still shook up from the jump, eh?"

Arka disregarded the comment and laughed to himself, now somehow hung up on the rules they had implemented long ago to avoid these very situations. Guess they forgot something along the way. He pondered how their rules applied in real life. They weren't just their own set of guidelines for journeying inward. One, leave no man behind. Two, never go it alone, always have people you can depend on in whatever rough time. Three, always have an exit, always have the means to shift your situation; never get stuck, know your options and be able to evaluate and overcome. And now the fourth: Have time, don't waste it. Use it to the best of your ability, and you will win the day.

This prospect was most directly conveyed through the age-old Latin cliché, *carpe diem*. If ever there was a spiritual gain or lesson to be learned from all of this, Arka staked his bet that it would be the canonizing of that very practice. He would take such to heart after this ordeal was over, as it all might truly prove a third-eye-opener. For you never know when the terminal journey will be upon you; never know when you'll cash your last check or disappear forever down a ravine of lava. He resolved to live each day to his fullest potential, always moving forward from here on out, striving to be better, fighting to accomplish, to create. This overlook riddled him with unbridled excitement and newfound confidence in the face of their current dilemma.

Brac aptly slapped Arka on the back and continued after Atris, who was now quite some distance ahead. They had made it off the charred plain to locate a path up one of the small foothills. Atris had claimed there was a plateau up ahead, and the archives were there, moving still to say it'd get them to the tower, and maybe the answers they were looking for.

Arka was admittedly suspicious of the sudden orientation his friend now possessed, but he had nothing else to go on.

"How do you reckon he knows where he's going so well?" he asked as he caught up to Brac.

Brac didn't break stride or line of sight, and was obviously not worried about it in the least. "I'm not worried about it in the least really. We don't have any better ideas, and it somehow feels right."

The mountain path leveled out and revealed a vast emptiness to their left.

"The ocean?" Arka speculated.

He and Brac made haste to Atris as he moved past the shielding barrier of the mountainside. The rocky landscape to their left had given way to gray vacancy over churning whitecaps a couple hundred feet below them. To their right now stood a smooth wall running perpendicular to the ground.

"Over here," Atris shouted back at them. They made their way along the flawless fortification until reaching its first abnormality in the form of a heavy iron door. Atris turned the handle, eliciting a shrill screech as the locking mechanism opened. He pushed the door inward and light hit their faces, bouncing up from the polished white floors within.

"Finally, some shelter." Brac pushed his way inside.

Arka hesitantly followed.

"We're here," Atris said.

★★★★

"We made it!" Aislin exclaimed as she deftly flew up the last stretch of stairs.

Nico was fatigued from the climb though in high spirits. It had been a fairly short venture through the woods to the base of the mountain, and it was only after the seemingly endless staircase embossed in its side that he felt any need for rest. It didn't matter much though. This girl, whoever she was, seemed to lighten his steps. Even during the uncertainty of the recent quake, they confidently waited it out, tucked safely within a sturdy ledge.

They had talked of several things throughout the trek. Nico even found himself embarrassed at times. He usually had a lot on his mind and was not one for insecurities. Whenever a Runner debate became too heated, he usually opted neutrality in light of his temper. He thought he might be growing too dissonant with society in general, losing interest in bitching about what matters they had no control over.

But this girl engaged his interests and drew out a wide range of intriguing conversation. She was attentive and compassionate, often pausing in their journey when she had something important to say. The only instance she wavered in her composure was during the discussion that had just transpired.

Nico laughed to himself, recalling it as he proceeded to the top of the stairs. He'd told her he was enjoying the journey as well as the mystery of it all, going on to say each of his days seemed to be getting more boring than the last anyway. Not one for shame or white lies, Nico further addressed the failing momentum of his brothers. He said the drugs weren't working for them anymore, and then laughed in spite of the statement's relative fallacy to the current situation.

Aislin knew what he was alluding to.

"Yes," she had said. "It does seem like every day wears on the same as the one before it. Perhaps that's why we resorted to dosing for all those years. We Runners thought there was a way to discover something inspiring by repeatedly diving into the recesses of our minds. What we didn't understand, was there's no great force waiting to make the connection with us, shake our hands and drag us along to some wondrous frontier. We are our own vessels; it is up to us and us alone to dispatch the onslaught of obstacles we encounter every day. Perspective Nico, the angle of attack is what matters. Whether it's dark days of lost faith – or rather the salad days, stints of rebirth – life is indeed a fight." She smiled brilliantly at the thought.

"Of course," Nico had said. "But where is the enemy? Boredom is not a tangible thing you can bludgeon. You can't help but get tired after a while."

Aislin smiled again. "The enemy?" she laughed. "–is gravity. We fight it each and every day. Think about the exertion it takes simply to latch onto something and leave the ground." She jumped up to grasp the branch outstretched overhead. "To hang in suspension, fighting against its relentless pull like an isolated banner at the mercy of the gale." She dropped back to the ground.

"Whatever poison you ingest day by day – whichever makes you feel best or helps you sleep at night, as they say. People drink all the time because it's the easiest way to cope with how monotonous life can get. It's imperative you never forget the fire, even if you feel you are going against the flow you hear others talk about. There are times to rest as well as times to beat yourself bloody upstream. A good life is a fight. Do something about it or spend your time putting yourself to sleep, waiting to die like all the rest."

Nico was invigorated. He felt like he had known her for much longer than a walk through the woods. It was irrational to feel so strongly for someone in such a short time, a girl he had only just met. He tried to dismiss the notion this was something he was going to be waking up from. The thought of their time together expiring had been banished from his mind. This beautiful girl had instilled a resilient sense of hope in him. It didn't matter if it was merely within this dream.

"Hey!" Aislin called warmly. "Did ya hear me? We're here!"

10

Time for flight in the black of night
of forgotten why, and battle cry;
time for change in the hearts of the proud
of revolution, and guns firing loud.
We took a chance, on a backwards glance
and no one cared for our final stance;
we travel on, without a sound
our hearts in hand, half past hallowed ground.

Nico reached the top of the stairs to see Aislin standing before a set of large iron doors.

"What is this place?" He gazed up at the enormous structure. The walls were two stories above their heads, chiseled perpendicular with the ground, devoid of a single blemish. Though his depth perception was finally improving with the coming dawn, he could barely make out another protrusion above, stretching into the sky from the building's roof. It couldn't be long now until the sun finally emerged.

"I'm sure it will be a beautiful day," Aislin said, as if detecting his thought. "I can't wait." She clasped the door handle and leaned back, the heavy iron slowly shrieking on its hinges.

Nico stared across the sky in the direction from which they'd climbed, still unable to see very far. There was a formidable amount of fog everywhere, blanketing the woods and plains below. He craned his neck up to see the moon directly overhead. Nico thought it odd, for it to still be so close, so prominent in the failing dark.

An abrupt gust triggered a complete cessation of the wind thereafter and a mounting chill came over him. He could hear a disturbance off to the left, followed by dislodged rocks rolling down the slope.

"Did you hear that?"

Aislin looked back from the threshold. Her face answered without words. Nico took a few steps toward the disruption. A thud emitted from around the corner of a large boulder, and the dark physique of a man came into view. He stood motionless, and was quickly joined by other silhouettes from around the craggy bend.

"Who's there?" Nico asked sternly, already certain the newcomers were aware of his presence.

Three of them slowly advanced on his position without a word. Nico adjusted his stance while the figures picked up speed. As they drew closer, he was unable to make out any discernable features. It was bright enough now, yet no characteristics were coming to light.

"That's close enough!" he shouted. He was never one to back down from a brawl. This quickly became no time for words. It was a time for fists.

"Nico!" Aislin screamed, pinned against the door, now only cracked open.

Two more figures, black as asphalt, had gotten behind him to move in on her. Nico charged at them, fastening a full-nelson hold from behind the first shape he reached, simultaneously swinging around to deliver a sidekick to the left torso of the other. There was a wisp of black dust, resembling ash in the wind, and the figure went sailing off the nearby drop. Nico held the other tightly, coping with the horrid realization that the form he was grappling bore no human characteristics – no hair, no clothes, no skin. This didn't change the objective. Nico's muscles tightened as the figure bucked its shoulders about. He wrenched right and heard the undeniable sound of snapping sinew. The figure in his grasp went limp.

Not a second later, Nico was gripped up from the side and whirled around as the three other humanoid shapes descended upon him. He looked forward. The head of his closest assailant was bereft any facial components. Instead, there was a recess, a cavity borne into the skull of whatever the hell this thing was.

Nico froze, locked in a stare with non-existent eyes. It was all he could do to keep his stance rigid against the force of the two attackers at his sides. He couldn't look away from the hollow head. His peripheral vision left him, and he was aware of a forward surge, the sensation of flying.

"They will try to lead you away." This voice was evil, raspy against an incessant low drone. Nico saw only what resembled television static that accompanied white noise.

"The illusion is almost over. There is no need to run," the sinister tone assured.

Nico was losing his immediate feeling, losing control.

"Things won't get any better back there." The low hum rose in volume.

"Countless others have contended these same problems to come up with no solution. Why bother fighting?"

"Nico!" Aislin's voice cut through the thick aura from what seemed a mile away. Nico was once again aware of his stasis. He recalled the yellow grass of the hill where she had found him.

"Hope." His diction had never been clearer. He seized his muscles again and braced hard to stay upright amidst a sudden pulling sensation, flying backward this time.

His vision returned. He was among two ashen shapes and the dissolving black magic, the hollowed skull in front of him once more. Nico tensed and lifted the rear attacker off the ground, simultaneously delivering his forehead into the other in front; closing his eyes to account for the ensuing cloud of ash.

"Aislin, run!" He grabbed the arm around him and broke free from submission, heaving the ash-man aside to skid off the cliff and into the abyss. He turned over his shoulder to see Aislin shim her way through the iron doors, evading the flailing arm of the last attacker as it tried to follow her. Nico stomped the figure recovering from the head butt, smashing what remained of its skull into the gravel. He ran to the threshold, brandishing his hardened shoulder and crashing into the partially open door. Another billow of ash fanned out as half of the assailant fell backward. A soft thud echoed from behind the recently shut doors.

Nico coughed amidst the permeating ash, wiping his face with his sleeve and catching his breath. He looked down at the halved creature. What were these things? They had the shape of something human, though that remained the only similarity. His head was cloudy, reminiscent the beginning stages of a bad hangover.

Things won't get any better? He mulled over the toxic words that echoed between his ears a moment ago. *What the hell?*

He stopped himself from harping on the madness and brushed his arms clear of layered ash as the growl of another rockslide emitted from around the bend. He held his breath and hastily creaked open the iron doors. The split remnants of the ash figure served to bar the handles once he was inside.

Nico made his way down a long hall, decently lit with repeating lanterns hanging at fifteen-foot intervals. Aislin was nowhere in sight. He felt slighted, but reasoned the inclination away. "Can't blame her for running," he whispered.

He briskly continued down the corridor upon the soft, royal blue carpet that stretched to the walls. It led to a vast room of white, littered with multitudes of tables and bookshelves. There was minor organization to the clutter, or at least there seemed to have been at one point. The shelves were indeed full, though without any clear regard for categorization. Several books were lying out on small mahogany tables, displaying pages of no obvious importance under the light of small desk lamps. The room possessed an overall feel of a neglected used bookstore well browsed over. Nico proceeded to one of the tables. The text upon it read simply:

Don't let yourself see you.

Aislin was still nowhere to be found. He moved to call out to her, but quickly reconsidered. This place was too foreign, and he didn't know enough about his surroundings to risk alarming someone – or any of those horrid ash-men for that matter.

★★★★

"I've been here before," Brac said as he gazed beyond the archway.

"Your turn to start remembering pieces of this puzzle," Arka gibed. "What is this place?"

"It's a library," Atris stated calmly as he walked past them, glancing left to an ascending spiral staircase before proceeding down the small vestibule as it gave way to a grand hall.

Brac and Arka curiously followed him out to the center of the room. There were shelves rife with books and loose writings, arranged in parallel fashion wherever they turned. An upper level boasted a sort of balcony that spanned all four walls of the immense chamber. Small lanterns hung from the walls, though they contributed little toward much of the area's details.

The primary light source was a roaring fire at the chamber's center. The blaze was set in the middle of a gigantic nautical star embossed in the granite floor. As if a defunct compass, its points all read "N," with a deep inscription etched into the outer ring housing:

The enduring, endless north, fueled by the boundless effort set forth.

A product of all our lessons learned. No loose ends, no chance of hostilities repelled and returned.

Utilizing experience to pass the test, laying ominous uncertainty to rest.

Striving through adversity, forged out of pain, for certain no loss can compare to such immeasurable gain…

The creed went on around the ring's circumference to the far side of the room. Brac crossed his arms and continued scanning their surroundings. Arka walked over to the nearest shelf and selected one of the hardbacks at eye-level. Atris chose another a few feet to the left. The sound of pages turning played against the marble.

"This – is my handwriting," Atris said uneasily.

"Are you surprised?" Arka's tone was reassuringly calm as he flipped through his own selection. Atris's eyes focused:

What is the measure of a man anyway? Is he his accomplishments in life?

Is he his legacy? His offspring? His stories and deeds?

Is he the mark left on the hearts of others?

Is he the comfort that watches over his dearest friends in times of darkness and doubt?

I believe, with solid conviction, that it is those who you cherish that will matter in the end. But where do we go from here exactly? Where is the light that shined straight through my mind in my days of unfathomable beauty? Where is that peace on my heart? The answer has to be in this place somewhere, perhaps below. ...

If I knew now, what I knew then.

Atris closed the bindings and returned the book to the shelf. "These are pretty interesting – too vague to help though. Brac?"

Brac was a few shelves down, intently examining pages of his own. "Yeah, I got nothing."

Atris cleared his throat, "That one said maybe something's below us."

"I thought we were making for the tower," Brac recapped.

Arka massaged his forehead. "...down stairs of glass," he mumbled.

"Stay with me bro," Atris remarked, passing on his right and making his way down the line of shelves. Rounding the corner to the left, he snagged another random volume from obscurity to accompany him as he meandered through the gridded halls. The pages were devoid of any markings. He was about to discard the book when ink suddenly appeared before his eyes, gracefully curling in lines of its own volition. The words rapidly unfolded an accounting of what seemed like someone's hunt for something...

> *I thought it was pretty funny how she said one could cover unspeakable distances in a single night. It makes total sense though, in light of the situation. I mean, where am I? Where did you go? And the hell were those things? This can't be all just a dream. I can feel it now. I can feel her, somewhere. And all these books, mostly nonsense, but still elaborate and complex. Aislin. Where are you?*

"Shit," Atris said.

Brac promptly came flying around the corner, "What is it? Figure something out?"

Atris presented the book for Brac's examination. "Is this your handwriting?"

"Definitely not," he answered. "Ha, can barely read my own. ... Arka's maybe?"

Atris spun the book around as the words continued to form on the page. "No. I'd recognize his anywhere. This is someone else – and he's looking for her."

> *I suppose this is all just what would be happening right about now. Suppose I'll wake up in the next few minutes. Dreams do usually end without any closure at all. I wonder if I'll remember*

her. Wait, who was that? Was it her? Another monster? No, some dude in black. Was that Arka? Looked too young. Should I follow? Damn, now who are these two?

Atris and Brac simultaneously looked up from the pages to see the dark outline of a man amidst the shelves at the end of the row. He stood unwavering, neither retreating nor advancing. Atris tucked the book under his arm.

Brac adjusted his stance for a potential tussle. "Oi!" he shouted firmly. "Who's there!?"

The shadow did not sway, but down the dim lit hall came a voice. "It's Nico."

"Well, I'll be damned!" Brac dropped both his guard and the air of tension. Atris recalled the name of another friend he had attended school with, though their relation was unremarkable aside from class intermissions. First Brac, now this guy? Nico walked up to them.

"So what is it you know?"

Brac laughed. "It's complicated, so not much. I got here, then there was a high dive, followed these guys up a river, then there was a hurricane, a cliff climb, raining fireballs, a near brush with a lava wave – all kinds of crap. ... Some of it was pretty badass actually. It's good to see another familiar face though. How'd you get here?"

Nico seemed somewhat perturbed at the mention of raining fire but must've deemed it illogical to pry into other's experiences in this place. "Well, I was in the woods, was with Ewan for a bit, then I met this girl. We came up the mountain and were ambushed by these weird-ass demon dudes. Got separated during the fight."

"Aislin," Atris said, too certain it was the name he would receive to bother posing it as a question.

Nico's eyes lit. "You know her?"

"I haven't seen her since the cliff house," Atris replied. "You said she's here? Is she all right?"

Nico shrugged. "She came inside, I know that much."

"Friend of yours then?" Brac asked. "Name doesn't ring a bell."

"Nah, just met her."

"Right," Atris said. "Wait, where did Arka get to?"

Nico pointed back and to the left. "Thought I saw him heading off that way, looked strange though."

"Strange how?" Brac asked.

"Everything comes off strange in this place," Atris snapped. "We've got to find everyone and get to the stairs."

"What stairs?" Brac questioned again.

"Well, let's split up and find 'em," Nico proposed.

The three nodded and fanned out through the grid of shelves, following Arka's apparent trajectory.

"Arka!"

"Aislin!"

"Ewan!"

No replies. Atris curiously removed the book from under his arm and once again parted its bindings:

>...*Like it really matters. He didn't say they were involved or anything. But that means she's not just a dream. Or does it? I feel so lost. Why do Atris and Arka look so strange? This has got to be all in my head. This is my crazy ass delusion and everyone*

else is here for the ride. But when will I wake up? Hopefully I
find her in time, if only to say goodbye.

Atris scoffed, unable to stifle a rising hint of jealousy. He wondered again how Nico was involved in all of this. He felt like he was an important piece to the whole puzzle, though couldn't help find it bizarre that someone he barely knew was in this crucial trip with him, whatever it meant. Perhaps more obscure acquaintances would start coming out of the shadows. And if they did, could he trust any of them?

He continued on in the search for his comrades, brushing aside any petty emotional discomfort. Atris was confident, the others had to be close by.

"Arka!" Brac called out, crossing Atris's path and disappearing behind another row of shelves.

"I saw him head over that way," Nico's voice sounded out from somewhere nearby. Atris rounded the corner after Brac and found him leaning over a banister, looking down on a lower level of the building. Multitudes of small candles hung from the ceiling above, their dim light barely revealing someone descend a grand marble staircase to the left of their position.

★★★★

"You heard that, right?" Ewan asked.

Arka was leaning over a small wooden table, rubbing the sides of his head again, "What?"

"Thought I heard your name," Ewan said, scanning the upper floor.

The duo had since left the tunnel behind and were inspecting their newfound stable setting. The descending spiral staircase in the center of the room granted passage into total darkness, hence written off as an option. And with Arka feeling faint again, he figured Ewan would yield to a few minutes respite before they moved on to the upper level.

"Headaches again?" Ewan questioned.

Arka turned and grunted. "Wish I could dream up a smoke."

"Yeah," Ewan agreed. "We should move on up soon. How do we get to the tower?"

"We have to find the others first. Can't leave anyone behind anymore." Arka was trying to concentrate on one of the open books spread out across the small table.

The second mechanism triggered is a faux sense that the new nightmare is the new physical world. After enough time, consciousness and subconscious begin to smear together and seemingly become one. Physical illusions are created: you might think you feel your bones heat up, the corners of the room start to appear as if they were licks of flames. —Terrifying mania throughout.

He shuddered, stung by instances of processes long and best left forgotten, aged trials he and his brothers had found themselves in a few times before – similar in many ways, night and day in others. He reassured himself that he still possessed too much voluntary control to worry about what the text was getting at happening to him. Courage, above all else.

Then he began to lose focus.

"Hey," Ewan whispered from behind. "Someone's coming down." He heard Ewan's footsteps shift and track to the broadside of the nearest bookcase.

"Yo!" Ewan shouted. Arka turned around.

"Wait – shit." Worry grasped Ewan's quivering voice. The newcomer made his way over to the glass staircase. Looking up, the light from above revealed his face. Arka froze, suddenly losing control of his movement. The figure hesitantly walked up to them.

"Shit!" he heard Ewan say again, this time with marked distress.

"Hey!" A voice echoed from somewhere to their left. *Atris?* The building started to tremble in a low roll.

"Damn it! Another quake!" *Was, that...Brac?*

"Arka!" Yet another different voice came from a figure hurdling down the marble stairs.

"Ewan! Get him back!" *...definitely Atris's voice.*

Arka couldn't see anything out of his peripheral vision anymore, his perceptions deafened and narrowed to the immediate scope of the figure directly ahead, and whatever madness now seizing control of everything he was.

"Told you, you should've stayed." The voice unmistakably belonged to Mary.

"You ready?" Greer asked.

Arka couldn't formulate any words to respond. He couldn't move. He felt the floor give in.

11

Herein lies a way out alive,
steep and sharp the narrow lane.
All we've attained up to this point,
has been a typhoon of the brain.
Yes, from here on out we'll bury doubt
to spin our tale from the inside out
to hit the shores knowing what's in store
to put to trial, this ongoing bout
'tween the two that are left, be it mind and breath.
A vow to you in me in true
and thus the whole is made anew,
a promise of penitence, a light drawn near
steadfast in our sentence, the answer lies in here.

Arka now perceived himself in total darkness, a low hum gradually rising in pitch ringing through his mind. He lifted his arms to see his hands before him, as if doused in sunshine, though there was no light source to speak of. Point of fact, there wasn't anything. He tried to walk forward, but there was nothing beneath his feet from which to push off.

"Should've known." Greer's voice again, this time further off.

A pinpoint of light came into view directly in front of Arka, closer by the second. It came up, straight to his eyes, then he swore he could feel a breeze. The low vibration occupying his mind came to an abrupt halt, replaced with the beautiful whisper of a low wind through healthy branches.

Well, that's a lot better. His thoughts sounded odd, as if he was observing himself as someone else or from some other point of perception.

"Yeah, it sure is," Atris said, passing him on his left. "We better get a move on though."

Arka glanced around wildly, finding he once more had control of his own cognition. He recognized his surroundings almost immediately. He was standing in the middle of a lush green field, about a perfect square quarter-mile, bordered by a dense tree line that danced in the noontime breeze of a warm spring. The sun was overhead. It seemed like it was the first time Arka had seen it in ages, and he spent a moment taking it in.

"You better catch up with the others." Greer's voice again, sounding calmly from all around him.

Arka whirled around, but saw nothing. Atris was already approaching the trees, indifferent, it seemed, to the presence of company.

"I can't stress enough," Arka's own voice played through his mind, causing him to lurch into pace, following after Atris.

He made it to the field's edge to find Ewan waiting there as well. His two friends looked strange. Their hair was longer, their clothes seemed slightly looser, and there was a glint in Atris's eyes that Arka had not seen for the longest time – a gleam all but forgotten. His creeping suspicion was validated as the next conversation unfolded.

"What an awesome day," Atris said, folding his arms. "I can't wait."

"Yeah, man." Ewan glanced over to Arka, frowning slightly. "You all right? Lookin' kinda spent."

"Never mind that," Atris said over his shoulder.

Arka paused for a moment. His words came naturally to him. "We have to keep moving if we are to get out of here and find the others."

"What?" Ewan questioned.

"Hah, right," Atris said with a laugh. "Things always did affect you first." He moved along the sun-kissed forest path.

Ewan scowled at Arka for a moment before doing the same. "Lightweight," he masked with a cough.

Arka couldn't help but laugh at the comment, despite his state of confusion. He remembered this place, this era even, and how his brothers looked. This had to be a distant memory of sorts.

The path wound along gradual bends and switchbacks, leading the boys through a verdant serpentine. Tall moss-ridden trunks loomed over beds of light-green ferns and underbrush, and the soft rhythm of packing soil crunched beneath their feet as the wind played Vivaldi through the leaves.

"Oi!" Atris shouted from the head of the small column.

Greer came down the path to meet them, healthy and whole. Arka felt faint.

"Anything from up ahead?" Ewan called out.

Greer ignored him and looked straight at Arka, "I thought I was with others, but it seems I've turned up alone. Did we come here together?"

"Don't know, but it's good we were here to pick you up." Atris said, shaking Greer's hand before starting down the path once more.

"Wait, hold on a second." Arka's wary smile faded as he mustered up a temporary cache' of courage. "Where are we going?"

Ewan just laughed and followed after Atris.

Greer motioned for Arka to follow suit. "Hopefully, it's somewhere we'd want to go."

Arka sighed. "As long as it's somewhere."

Within a few minutes of traversing the woods, the boys found themselves making their way down a stretch of train tracks; Atris in the lead, followed closely by Ewan, with Greer keeping carefree pace alongside Arka at the rear.

"Hey, you get the feeling you've been here before?" Greer quietly asked Arka.

"Don't even!" Atris shouted from the front. Arka was off-put, chills of paranoia starting to form again. There was no way Atris could have heard the question from so far away. Perhaps he was just talking to Ewan. He glanced over to see if Ewan was readying a response, but was met instead with a hard stare.

"Look on the bright side," he said in a reassuring tone. "This may turn out to be quite the story."

Arka had little time to analyze any rising suspicions of conspiracy, his worries instead turned to the steadily intensifying rattle of the tracks beneath their feet. The others felt it as well, halting in step.

"Let's jump this thing," Atris confidently proposed. "We'll get to the hill a lot quicker."

"Man, hell with that. It doesn't feel like a crawler," Ewan deduced.

Greer's voice was monotone and calm, "Nothing but slow crawlers going through this stretch, Ewan. Shouldn't be a problem."

Within seconds, Arka saw the train lean 'round the bend, about 400 feet away. It was undoubtedly an express, and the boys stepped back to the shelter of the woods – all except Greer.

"Hey!" Arka shouted. "Forget it, man. It's way too fast!"

The train's whistle sounded as it drew near. Greer didn't flinch. Arka pressed hard to launch himself back up the small rocky incline to the tracks, but was restrained from behind, blackened arms around his neck and waist, ash filling his nostrils. The rocks around them vibrated, and the metal rails whined. The whistle sounded again. Greer stood a statue. Arka struggled free from the bind, whirling around to see a dark fist flying straight at him as the speeding train thundered by.

Darkness again.

"That all you got?" A familiar voice broke through the stinging sensation in his mind.

Arka stumbled and opened his eyes. There was asphalt beneath his feet, and the unmistakable chill of winter air around him, beaten away in flash waves of heat from the nearby crackling of a small bonfire.

The solid strike had knocked his vision to a blur. He hesitated, then wiped a spot of blood from his lip. Arka found stable footing and focused his eyes, honing the adrenaline flow. A sense of familiarity befell him once more.

Brac stood before him, allowing his opponent chance to regain his stability after that last blow. Arka's vision darted wildly about, and he brought his guard up to find gloves covering his hands. Suddenly confident, he charged in on a natural whim, landing a solid strike to Brac's chin. Brac quickly shook it aside, and the boys parried off. Their fists wildly found their marks, sounding out as if the frosty forest was coming down around the asphalt slab.

But was it? The pronounced sound of cracking wood could be heard from off in the distance, and it was growing closer. Arka looked toward the steady blaze off to the left. Through the rising rays of heat he could see Atris on the far side, bottle of whiskey in hand, sitting next to a girl with ashen-blonde hair.

"Arka!" Ewan shouted from off to his right, shocking him back to full awareness only too late to defend against Brac's left hook, which hit him square in the jaw and spun him round and off his footing. Arka felt his legs go.

He folded on the ground with a soft rustle amidst the underbrush, moving next to shuffle behind a large bush on the side of a brick house. The comforting heat of the fire had vanished, though so had the frigid air that called for it. It was now a warm, dark night, with only the dim streetlights presenting a common neighborhood avenue thirty feet from his new hiding place.

Arka caught his breath and rubbed his jaw, tucking his legs closer into concealment in order to evade a searchlight that suddenly pierced the night from someplace down the street. He turned aside just as a 150-pound missile-made-Ewan shot up from the shadows and onto the six-foot fence to his left, bucking his legs in a lurching motion and disappearing over the far side. The searchlight reactively traced the ruckus, giving Arka the gripping signal the game was afoot. Overwhelming confusion be damned, he was fairly certain that whatever foe was upon them, detection meant disaster. He deftly whirled around and hopped the fence after his fleeing brother, falling over the other side.

He splashed down into the softness of a murky swamp, mud reaching up to consume his feet and hope for his ankles. Only the pale light of the moon overhead and a few scattered traces of luminescence from distant streetlights cut through the wood.

No bearings at all this time. Not even the fence behind him, no menacing searchlight to his six. He sighed and tried to steady his heart, which was flying a mile a minute.

"All right, relax. Think." Arka resorted once more to their key strategy of dealing with a panicked state of solace.

This new environment bore no discernible indications of where he might be. No landmarks or familiar stand-out trees.

"No. Don't lose your head."

He started off through the low muck, which was nearly impossible to walk through. Was he near the pits? Had that been it? Had he just woken up from all this madness?

The lights. *Not again!*

Several beams cut through the forest to find him. Arka flew, practically skipping atop the mud, aptly dodging roots and low-fallen branches reaching out to ensnare him. The sticks strained to mark his face with their spiteful brand, ever dense and more diligent as he boldly charged on. The rays of light hit the trees in front of him, and everything around was consumed by a brilliant white.

It permeated all he was for a moment, but it wasn't long before Arka made out discernible features again, coming out of the radiance.

He was standing in a white room, with but a single window to the left, and a door a few feet away that swung silently ajar on its hinges. His body tensed, and he positioned his arms up to his chest, readying his guard for whatever insane pseudo-memory trial was about to present itself next.

Nothing.

Furious, he sprang through the doorway and into a corridor lined with a burgundy carpet covering the wood flooring that creaked beneath his feet. He could feel a draft down the hall, smell the nylon fibers that made up the rug. He squinted, adjusting his eyes to the dim light produced by repeating lamps hanging from the walls.

"Might as well see if I can find the books." The rough voice came from behind him.

Arka spun around, fist cocked back, just in time to see Ewan disappear around the corner about twenty feet away. Arka took after him, rounding the junction to find an empty hall. He turned to the door at his right, a faint laugh emitted from within its frame. It suddenly flung open with great force, sailing into his forehead and sending him sprawling to the carpet. His eyes went fuzzy.

"Don't even." Atris said from nearby. "Look on the bright side."

Arka's vision faltered and vied for focus. He staggered to his feet and peered down the hall again. A figure faded into form, with another right behind him, then another. The corridor was instantly occupied by blurry renditions of himself, as if his trip down the hall was expressed in a visible pattern.

"This may turn out–"

Everything faded to black again.

"Get him back!"

His head was pounding as his vision progressively adjusted once more. He now sat in the driver's seat of some foreign car, nestled downward at a 45-degree angle in a ditch, one remaining headlight illuminating only what immediate inches of dirt it could penetrate. Arka furiously smashed the steering wheel and sounded the car's pitiful whining horn.

"What the shit!? I don't even drive!" He was shouting at no one in particular, maddening confusion ringing throughout the automobile's tattered upholstery. It was up there on the list of last places he expected to find himself next. He hated cars even, always referring to them as death-traps or expensive wastes of time, despite how asinine the point of view usually came across to his friends.

"Maybe this is why you don't."

Arka looked up into the remnants of the rearview mirror to see Greer sitting peacefully, carelessly looking out the side window as if they were cruising down some rural highway on a hot summer afternoon. Arka's sight left the mirror, and he aggressively turned around. The backseat was empty.

"That figures."

The door was crunched inward, so he climbed his way into the backseat and kicked open the rear driver-side door, ultimately falling into the embrace of soft soil. He stood up and climbed onto the level plain of a dirt field, the stretching twilight revealing a few silhouettes a stone's throw off. They were staring up at the moon, which was centered within a massive halo of light.

Arka made his way over in a brisk walk, breathing heavy in his intensifying frustration. As he drew closer, he counted two figures standing, and five others sitting cross-legged even further ahead. The air ahead was rife with trace light waves ranging of all colors, as if there were unperceivable surfaces all around serving as prisms.

"Right. Hello." He couldn't think of anything else to say upon approaching the standing pair.

The light of the full moon revealed the face of Greer, the other Mary's.

"What's going on?" Arka prayed he would get some sort of helpful answer, though he expected otherwise. "This nightmare is getting old."

"We tried to wake up for so long," Mary said solemnly as she lowered her lock-stare from the sky. A green aura flowed around her.

Greer didn't bother looking down. "It really is irrelevant."

"No." Arka turned to Mary. "Juli, which is the way out?"

She smiled and touched the side of his face with icy fingers. "We cancelled the restart, you and I. We stopped the sun from coming up, we reconfigured–"

"That's enough." He recoiled from her, turning next to Greer. "Brother, I know you must be more than just a trick of the mind. Help me. Please." Arka's aggravation gave way to humility.

Greer broke his own sky-locked stare and came to look upon Arka, with pearl-white eyes devoid of iris or pupil, "You know what lies ahead. You've been there before."

The sight frightened Arka, still he tried to stitch together the seams of his failing composure. "How do I get back?"

"Back home then?" Greer questioned.

"Yes. How long until this is over?"

"I wish I knew." Greer slowly returned his sight to the sky.

Mary whimpered. "It feels like I have been here for so long already, but I don't rightly recall just how we all got here."

"We are all headed to the same place," one of the figures seated up ahead called back in an unrecognizable voice. "North." A silhouetted arm extended toward the horizon.

Arka looked in the presented direction, then up at the entrancing moon overhead. Sighing heavily, he returned his attention back to the matter at hand, only to now find himself suddenly amongst a multitude of strangers. He looked about frantically. Everyone was dressed in black, gazing remorsefully at the white carpet now beneath his feet. The air in the room was thick with despair. Following trending stares, his gut wrenched when he realized where he was, as two people stepped away from the tempered wooden box on display at the front of the room. The casket was of fine oak, roses and laurels adorned the platform it rested upon, and in it lay the body of his friend.

"No – not. Why?" He questioned aloud.

No one heeded his vague inquiry. A torrent of memories flooded back to Arka as he fell to his knees and cradled his head in his hands. "No. Not again," he pleaded.

He stifled his rising anger and staggered to his feet to find he was alone once more.

The funeral procession was gone, along with the room itself. There was nothing discernible on the dark horizon. The moon revealed disturbances and shimmers occurring about the ground, reflecting the heavens above in mirror-lake fashion, drawn out in various shades of deep blue.

Arka massaged his forehead and studied his footing, sure enough observing ripples as he lifted his feet.

"Great. ... And next I meet Jesus."

A rumble came from below and sent a high undulation out from where he stood.

"The enduring, endless north, fueled by the boundless effort set forth." Atris's voice came from somewhere close by, projected in the manner of dictating to an auditorium.

"A product of all our lessons learned," Ewan's tone took over. "No loose ends; no chance of hostilities repelled and returned."

"Utilizing experience to pass the test, laying ominous uncertainty to rest," Nico's voice added.

"Striving through adversity, forged out of pain, for certain no loss can compare to such immeasurable gain." *Brac?*

"Veiled opportunity to raise the whispered above the common dream, a celebration of beauty only few have seen." That was certainly Juli.

Arka feverishly scanned the area, discovering not a single visual indication anyone was around him.

"For it's northbound on to the enduring force, with conviction and clarity to hold steady our course." Greer's voice again filled the air.

"With strength of heart and love for free will, do the Runners set brooding opposition up for the kill." *Who was that?*

Arka argued his mind was simply distorting all these voices into more familiar tones. Wherever he was, he doubted anyone speaking to him was doing so in the conventional sense.

"For it's imminent war we are training." He turned to see himself, plain as day, a mirror image acting of its own volition. "It's the beast within we are taming."

Arka swallowed his fear, gazing into this self-rendition. He replied confidently, "And our battle cries echo on northward still."

He felt a cold chill, and gravity seized his frame. He was pulled down, falling through open space instead of aquatic suspension. Gradually his freefall slowed and in the next second he felt he was drifting upward. Curves of blue-lit stone came into view amongst a pending dawn. He was levitating just off the ledge of a spire that wound skyward around a wide center column. A colossal oak was pedestaled atop the structure.

"Shit!" He heard Ewan's sharp voice echo from around the bend, followed by the loud drawn-out groan of a compromised wood structure.

Arka was in a state of weightlessness, unable to move away from or toward anything. He looked up to the moon, directly overhead, appearing five times its normal size. He next surveyed the situation below, noting a roof of glass encasing several small light sources inside a massive building.

"Get him back!" Atris's voice boomed through the sky.

Arka suddenly felt heavy, as if he was being pulled down and to the left by some sort of vacuum.

"Come back for us!" His friend's voice resounded once more, from a different point than before. Arka felt the weight intensify and begin to press against his chest. He went to scream but couldn't. He was falling again.

★★★★

"Anything yet?" Nico asked in desperation.

"Not a damn thing!" Ewan said. He was hunched over Arka, striking him wildly in the chest in an overhand ax fashion.

"I don't think that's how you do that," Brac said as he stood over them.

"Shut up, man! The hell are you anyway?" Ewan angrily snapped.

"He's right. You're not going to get him back like that. Think he's just going to cough it up or something?" Atris was leaning over a nearby reading table some ten feet away, flipping through page after page.

"And the hell with me for trying then!" Ewan said sarcastically. "– should just be sitting around reading bullshit."

Atris had chosen the route of patience since Arka collapsed, resorting again to sift through the boundless literature around them, combing every leaf for some shred of an answer to –well, anything. He browsed through myriad topics ranging from a list of known astrological paradigms to a case study on sunlight. Halting his search, he reached over to the book he had brought down the stairs with him, opening its pages to the current end as it continued on still.

Man, he better wake up soon. We aren't getting anywhere now. I don't want to leave, but I have to find her. We all have to stick together though, right? What if those things come back? …But this is my dream, so if I leave, none of this nonsense here will really be happening. That's how this works, right? Or maybe these guys are questioning if I'm really here as well.

Atris let out a slight laugh, which his company ignored like the half-dozen before it.

Maybe she's down those stairs that Arka was heading toward, the ones Atris keeps looking at. Is he actually figuring anything out from these things? This is such a mess.

"She's not," Atris said aloud.

"What?" Brac turned and asked, being the only one within immediate earshot.

Atris closed the book. "Nothing, just–"

"His eyes!" Ewan shouted. Arka started gasping. His friends all rushed to his side, as he sprang up to a seated position, striking Ewan in the ear.

"What?" he started. "…What?"

"Wish we knew," Brac said.

"You saw yourself," Atris assured. "You all right?"

"I … I think so," Arka replied, taking Brac's hand and rising to his feet. He cautiously looked about the room, all of his friends were there, happy to see him. He stared hard at Atris smiling back at him.

"Glad to have you back, man."

Arka hesitated for a moment and suppressed something that was obviously troubling him. Everyone knew it must be whatever trauma he had just gone through. He sighed heavily and looked at the floor. "We need to get to the tower. Up above. ... Sun's coming. Not much time left."

"Right, there's something I have to check first," Atris said, gaining prompt attention and following stares from everyone in the room. He looked over to Nico, knowing he was hoping to hear Aislin's name without reading it in the text.

"Never mind, it's nothing," he lied. Only Arka seemed to detect it as such.

"Right, we make for the roof. Let's get a move on!" Brac moved to rally his brothers.

"Why the roof?" Nico questioned.

"Just trust me, I've seen it," Arka said indignantly, somehow completely collected, renewed from the preceding ordeal. He followed Brac toward the marble stairs, Ewan close behind. Atris and Nico brought up the rear.

The five tired travelers made their way through the halls of the library with notable haste. Atris couldn't get his mind off the glass stairs. It was as if something or someone was reaching out to him. They were still without Aislin, and he couldn't leave her behind if they found a way out. Something told him she wasn't going to show up along the way to the tower either. He had to make a move, and quick, but how could he without jeopardizing the others?

"Listen," he whispered to Nico. "I'm going after Greer. There's not enough time to find both him and Aislin. Too much ground to cover."

Nico was intrigued and lowered his ear slightly, "Going after *who?*"

"Greer is down those stairs. Aislin has got to be somewhere else as well."

"How do you know?"

Atris turned to his side and pulled the book from under his arm. "I've read it," he said shrewdly. "...Prove it," Atris read aloud. "What are you waiting for? ... No way, he has to be full of – but, ostriches."

Nico stopped dead in his tracks.

"Blue," Atris continued, not looking up from the book. "Yellow, broken star, lasers. Shit. How–"

"All right, enough!" They both said simultaneously.

Atris shut the book and backed away. "If this is your dream Nico, then go find Aislin." He turned and made a full sprint back the way they came.

★★★★

"Oi, keep up!" Brac's voice rang from somewhere up ahead. Nico watched Atris retreat and hastened back to the others. He rounded the corner and nearly collided with Arka, who had come bounding down a flight of narrow stairs.

"Where's Atris?" Arka asked immediately.

Another slight rumble sounded below and the whole building shook for a split second, the aftershock dying down with the rising anxiety it had instantly stirred in their hearts.

Nico recoiled, "He went back for Greer?"

"What?" Arka bellowed, knowing Nico was unfamiliar with the name. "Shit! I knew it."

Brac and Ewan had backtracked down the stairwell to rejoin them.

Arka grunted, "All right. Brac, continue to the roof with Ewan and Nico. Ewan is already up there repairing the lift. He'll need your help."

"...But Ewan's right here," Nico said.

Ewan conveyed slight worry as he realized what Arka was getting at, "No…he means."

"Right, well we don't have time to mull it over now do we?" Brac asked irritably. He hesitated, in spite of doubt himself. "But what if I run into another me?"

"You won't," Arka assured him. "You and Nico have only been here a few times."

"Okay, hold on, I got something," Nico jumped in. "What if you aren't really here? Who's to say any of this is happening on any set reasons?" He stepped back from the group and readied his guard, shifting his eyes around as if he had just gotten to the bottom of this whole complex mystery.

"Not now, Ace!" Arka countered, insulted by Nico's strategy. "Attempting to change the direction of this nightmare by challenging the flow is not going to get us all out of this one. –bit more complicated at this point, and we need to work together."

The tension was palpable.

"Right, well–" Ewan started.

"Just get to the roof! Atris and I will be coming up just shy the end," Arka ordered. He took off back toward the lower hall. Brac was already making for the upward path. Ewan turned to Nico, who, for some reason, had begun frantically shuffling through the nearby shelves.

"Let's go dude!" Ewan pleaded.

"I'll catch up." Nico responded, unmoved.

"The fuck is going on all the sudden!?" Ewan shouted to the ceiling. "We were so close!" He lowered his eyes back down the hall. "First rule." He reluctantly turned from the ascending stair and took flight after Arka.

12

The sand gave way beneath their feet as the darkness swallowed what was left of the sun. The fire bound between them, it'd seemed like forever since the time they tried to run. We must never be afraid.

There is formidability everywhere outside the doors of your immediate life and each day may bring a colder, darker fight.

We must sift out idle hours and suicide the parts of me that cling to ways of our old lives that anchor us in a stagnant sea.

As the seasons teach us the mystery of our years, floating in space on a turbulent sphere, we must answer every new day with a renaissance of our breath, for you never remember the stories of those who gave up and turned back.

Atris was upon the lower hall once more, setting foot onto the descending stairs of glass. The archives' vast catalogues had provided him with none of the answers he sought, making the descent a necessary move at this point. He had little idea what waited in the darkness below. All he knew, all he felt rather, was that Aislin was down there. He felt his brothers were close to discovering a way out of this illusion, but he wasn't about to leave without the girl. He had grown up playing too many Nintendo games and rescued far too many pixelated princesses.

"Atris." Her voice was made a whisper, carried up on a slight draft from the depths.

Atris tossed the book under his arm aside and went over to the wall, rubbing his palms together. He jumped up and grasped the protruding steel neck of the mounted lantern. The small metal cage moaned under his weight before snapping at its foundation, sending Atris back to the floor.

He got up and centered the candle, thankful what bit of spilt wax failed to smite the flame. He undid his belt and tugged it from his pant loops with a zip-line sound, wrapping it around itself and fashioning the cloth into a handle through the hot circular ring on the lantern's topside. Atris turned, made his way to the center of the room, and descended the glass stair.

★★★★

"Damn." Arka allowed his waist to hit the banister, observing a dim light fade into the center recess in the level below. He looked to his left and saw Ewan vaulting down the stairs, landing with a roll on the hard floor of the lower hall.

"Damn!" He took off for the staircase himself. "Ewan! Hold up!"

Ewan saw Arka come up behind him and stopped shy of the glass stair. "He's down there, right? I just saw him go." Ewan struggled to catch his breath. "What's down there?"

A loud bang echoed off the marble from the main hall above. It sounded twice more, resonant of ringing iron.

"The hell was that?" Ewan asked.

Arka set foot onto the first step. "I've no idea, but you better get to the roof."

"Yeah, right," Ewan scoffed. "Like I'm really the rookie you been calling me all this time, even after I tried to save your ass from that crazy chick. You're not going this one alone, man."

Arka couldn't help but smile. He had no ammunition to counter. Ewan was always stubborn, and arguing would only delay them further. "Let's go get 'em then." The two made their way down, with the light of the archives dying out in the shadows. Arka stepped off the stairs onto solid ground, black as obsidian, Ewan close behind. They made for the lone flame floating precariously up ahead.

"There he is," Ewan said, running quickly toward the light. Arka followed.

Atris stood silent, holding the lantern before him as if studying phantom hieroglyphics in some ancient tomb.

"Hey!" Ewan shouted. "Asshole! What're you doing? We gotta get outta here."

"Come on, let's go back," Arka urged.

"I can't yet," Atris replied, uncertainty in his voice. "She's here. ... Somewhere."

"This is just a spooked-out hole of a basement," Ewan said. "No one's down here. Let's bail."

A stiff gust suddenly tore through the void and directly up the spines of the three wanderers. The dim flame in Atris's lantern flickered wildly and went out.

"...Anyone got a lighter?"

Ewan laughed. They couldn't see a thing. The only visual reference was the light playing off the edges of the opening above.

"No choice now," Arka said. "Let's move." He started for the stairs just as a fire broke out before him, throwing light thirty feet into the shadows.

★★★★

Ewan jumped back, shielding his face with his sleeve as the fire gradually became tame. "Well, now there's that," he said from behind cloth. He turned to see Atris standing there stoic, looking into the blaze.

Ewan was perplexed, noticing Atris's appearance had changed significantly in the flash of the fire. It was as if his face had aged, his hair was considerably shorter, and he was clad in a white shirt instead of a black hoodie. His folded arms bore jet black markings Ewan had never seen before.

He was smiling gently. "Ewan. ... You came back."

Arka and Atris made their way around the fire to where Ewan stood with the figure in white. Seeing his brothers approach, Ewan realized what was about to happen and leapt directly over the blaze to intercept them.

"Atris, get out of here," he pleaded.

"Why? Who's that?" Atris looked ahead to see his image coming around the tall flames.

"You all came back." His own voice, sure enough.

Arka grabbed him and started for the stair but Atris threw him off.

"Hold on!" he said, staring back at this aged rendition of himself, who appeared just delighted in the wake of the last few seconds' events.

Ewan stood beside him, leaning back to help Arka to his feet, "Why isn't he freaking out like you did, with the statue deal and the falling to the floor and what not?"

"Because of Conscious Fusion," the new Atris said excitedly. "No need to worry about the intimidating process of projectile recognition; two conscious states of the same timeline colliding ...and what not. We have complete control down here."

Arka reluctantly lowered his guard and gave up trying to pull his brother out of this conversation. Ewan wasn't so sure.

The aged Atris continued, "We three veterans have trained enough to traverse the dreamscape as only two separate forms. That was an arduous task, getting it down to that. But it's so good to actually see you two, just in time for another set no less."

"Just in time? A set? We've got to get out," Ewan implored.

"Nah," the older Atris played it off. "You made it this far. Now we can get at construction again." He received no trace of the comprehension or excitement he was probably hoping for from Ewan, or from his younger self for that matter.

"Have it make sense," young Atris demanded.

"Right!" the other shouted excitedly, the nearby flame roaring with his outburst before dying down to near embers. "Conscious Fusion is born of our mind's translation of our existence on this plain, in order to conform to the physics we grew up with. We see ourselves as individual renditions because we are more comfortable seeing such singularities."

Young Atris took a step closer. "But there are two of us. And there were two of Arka."

His aged variant seemed encouraged upon the rebuttal, "And I trust Arka had a massive recollection upon the collision of his timeline?"

Arka remained silent.

Aged Atris continued, "True, we couldn't reduce it to less than a pair, as both stages represent ourselves at both points of detachment."

Ewan turned to the stairs, growing increasingly wary they would soon vanish. "Points of detachment from what?" he asked over his shoulder.

"From time, Ewan."

"...All right," Ewan conceded. "So all of this is happening in a night or something? Whose dream is it? How is it we all have control? How is it a shared hallucination?"

"It's not a hallucination, not in the conventional sense," aged Atris replied. "This is real, just not when evaluated under your current allocations of reality." He was met with three following stares. "Think of it in historical terms."

"Shit," Ewan said under his breath.

Atris continued, "See, ages before we grew up, mathematicians pursued an understanding of the world around them: basic number theory, geometry, and algebra for instance, each building up successively of course. As mankind progressed, with technological advancements we were able to grasp evermore complex sciences in pursuit of the unknown. The unknowns, of course, are what change."

The fire danced back to life again.

"We've evolved thus far based upon the presumption that time is linear. Why it's only been just over a century since our civilization began to grasp relativity."

"Okay, Time dilation stemming from Einstein's theory of relativity," young Atris followed. "How time is perceived via different angles, thus proposing the existence of infinitely varying occurrences of space and time. Though what difference does it make? We still form our own definitions of now, just as you said regarding Conscious Fusion."

Ewan glanced at the opening in the ceiling again. "We sure are wasting a lot of time talking about it."

"Don't worry, brother, we are exempt down here," old Atris moved to settle Ewan's worry. "There is pure freedom here. No laws, no restrictions, no influence."

Arka broke his silence, "How is it you're here?"

Atris's aged-self laughed. "The same way we all are: the spike."

"The what now?" Arka came off unimpressed.

"The spike, an anomaly in the fabric of space-time. ...You see, we've made it through to the other side, detached from the shared consciousness of the earth, freed from the restraints of a linear existence."

"No way, we gotta get to the tower so we can wake up," Ewan said.

"We have already woken up," old Atris cut in. "Time is the friction that slows our conscious thought down to discernible matter. It's what gives us the perception of a beginning and an end, of durations and progressions, a useful force indeed – though humankind is hindered by an inability to progress beyond the simplified rendition we have known thus far. There is not enough cooperative focus. There are too many distractions, excessive material glorification, too much selfishness, conflict and war born of apathy, intolerance, and fear. Time is a stock-taking. We have transcended this."

"I sure as hell don't think I've transcended fear," Ewan said.

"You can here, Ewan. We all can."

"We can't stay here, Atris," Arka pleaded.

"You still haven't explained how we got here," Atris's younger self said calmly.

"Of course, the spike. As far as I've researched it must have been a sort of quantum vortex that radically manipulated the linear flow of our natural lives. The points of detachment are two separate points of our lives at the leading and trailing edge extremes of the spike – what you perceive as a younger and older self. ... You can't honestly still believe we are all just tripping."

Ewan digested Atris's pitch, "So we're in a wormhole?"

"I like to think of it as more of a funnel, or a spire," Atris said confidently.

"What would cause such a thing?" Ewan asked.

"Just what is it you think we're doing here?" Arka interrupted.

"What we've endlessly talked about in the past, brother. We are creating our own world – one not plagued by the squalors of man and the sins of our forefathers; one not swayed by innate human depravities that have caused an absolutely immeasurable amount of suffering throughout history. You see, it's in this manner our kind may have started, in a very similar moment of rally to realization. Whatever force initially utilized the energy of the universe for vast construction, it can be our turn now!"

"Then why haven't you gotten started yet?" young Atris asked, apparently growing impatient in the face of his aged self's rhetoric.

Aged Atris smiled, as if he had been anticipating the very question. "Well, I've been waiting for all the right variables. You see, it's been difficult, with the barriers presented by Conscious Fusion and the matter of getting our collective wit and energy on the same page, if you will." He turned away from the dim fire and looked out into the black.

"You see boys, we all are one, and our aim is to transcend, even if you still feel you should hold onto the old world. Why do you think you came back for me?" He paused, though not long enough for anyone to conjure up a feasible answer.

"Certain things are meant to be. We spent so much time in this dreamspace, amassing it all, documenting everything through our perceptions of humanity, and we have it all up there."

He whirled around and pointed to the staircase.

"We have suffered much, mostly at our own hands and foolish curiosity. Though no great thing is ever gained without substantial risk, no measure of triumph is attained without account for sacrifice. There's but one factor imbedded deep in our behavior proving the most resilient to eradicate.

We have cycled through all the emotions the brain can deliver. Heed all the channels we have traveled through to get here – the old world we knew, the dose, the halo, the lights, the journey across the scape above – finally arriving here in this sanctum of the mind.

This journey has hit elevated heights of enlightenment at times, true to speak. However, it's been fear, primal fear that always proves the prevailing emotion of the human condition. It's the very first thing you are born with. What could be more traumatic than existing for nine months in total warmth, experiencing little to nothing, only to be ripped away from it all? –To be thrown into complete disorientation, forced to start your lungs for the first time as you undergo a barrage of foreign sensory stimulations?

The brain knows fear first, from the instant your senses are activated – perhaps even sooner. Love comes second. A lot of people can live their lives without love, though everyone feels fear. ...See, first we Runners had to fully understand it, to dissect all the places we've been within and, in turn, overcome this daunting force altogether."

Atris paused, granting Arka an opportunity to cut in for counter's sake. "And dissect it we did," he affirmed. "But it just can't be done. Rigid fear is the most fierce and effective of tools. It is programmed into what we are. Think of all it has wrought throughout history. In the human body, calling on true, archaic fear is the last resort against a wandering mind about to make its terminal escape. You know this. They were your writings, I recall. Should the mind, in its entirety – subconscious and conscious states alike – separate from its vessel completely, the body would shut down involuntary life-sustaining functions."

Ewan was both empowered and off-put by his brother's sudden fever pitch.

Arka went on, "Pure, digging fear is utilized at the edge of this process of complete severance, at the point of no return, in order to keep the mind and body alive." Arka's last words came hard.

Ewan sensed mounting tension and chimed in, "And you were always the one talking about the balance of the universe. We need to get back to reality Atris. *This* is all an illusion. There's no life down here. And there needs to be fear to contrast love, wrongs to measure the rights. Misfortunes must riddle life to elevate wondrous occurrences in standing."

Arka scowled. Young Atris cut in, "We figured out why this was happening, remember? Our brains have been utilizing only their subconscious areas for too long, at an accelerated rate to allow construction of this scape. If our conscious selves fail to break away from this delusion before the meshing of consciousness and sub is complete … well, we're just locked here. The process is what we keep running from in this world, from the moment we leave reality. It's time running out of us, the intangible hourglass draining since the lights first brought us here."

His aged-self laughed dismissively. "I know it seems that way at first, but you will come to realization. The mind can do anything within itself. It's our worldly senses that can prove an enemy, our tether to the ground."

Arka seemed unmoved. "What caused the quantum spike?" he asked while looking at his feet.

Aged Atris smiled. "I haven't figured that out yet. It's not a stretch to imagine that we were all somehow tuned into the event, targeted even, by some force. Individual human perception is likened to a small frequency receiver, capable only of interpreting small messages taken from an infinite field of conscious occurrences. Perhaps the dose aided in allowing us to perceive a doorway leading off the linear map or gave us just the right mix of intuition and fortune to stumble upon the very precise point in space-time where the vortex occurred."

"The pits?" Ewan asked in a whisper.

"Perhaps," Atris answered. "Now that you guys are here, we can amass a vessel of consciousness. This may be our interdimensional threshold.

"Just how long have you been here?" Arka asked, a hint of agitation in his voice.

"It's impossible to say, Arka. There is no concept of the time we knew here. There is but a curtain born of the laws we grew up with. Time is not constructed of a standard linear model; instead, just as everything else in nature, it follows more of a fractal correlation. If we can uncover what caused our severance from our initial partition of time—"

"I know what caused it," Arka interrupted.

Aged Atris didn't attempt to mask his excitement. "This is what I'm talking about! You guys came back because that's what we always did for each other. And now, now we can share in this monumental journey just like the small iterations in time when we were kids!"

Arka clenched his fist and looked up at Atris. "It was you."

Atris smiled and took a few steps closer.

"Well I suspected that might be so, it's just a matter of uncovering and understanding how the phenomena occurred at those precise points in space and time."

"The precise location," Arka said slowly. "Halfway between the points of detachment on the linear model. Halfway between the earliest and the latest perceived renditions of ourselves in this dreamscape. ...When you died."

As if the words were a warhead set off on a distant fault line, the boy's footing slowly became unstable, coupled by an unnerving rumbling sound resonating from above.

"You can't honestly believe that!" Ewan shouted. He went to grab Arka and make for the stairs but faulted and fell to the ground as the shaking intensified. Atris and Arka were facing each other, levitating in the air. Everywhere Ewan looked he saw his brothers, different renditions varying in appearance and adhering to a wave-like pattern that followed milliseconds delayed motion to the adjacent instance. They occupied as far as Ewan could see, and he strained his eyes shut, feeling about the ground for stable footing.

He backed up and bumped into someone behind him. Greer stood there with his arms crossed, a blank expression on his face housing clouded eyes.

"You guys must choose," he turned to face Ewan. "Everything is falling apart."

Ewan quickly turned away, repeatedly denying the near-certainty he'd just seen a ghost. He thought back on Atris's unfolding grandiloquence, along with Arka's frightening claim and his confidence upon stating the notion. Ewan resolved to remain stoic. Through one open eye he saw young Atris vanish entirely. The last shred of comforting light from the upper level dimmed to total darkness.

★★★★

Arka was reeling for control over the rampant mania that had erupted around him. His vision shot all over the place, unable to focus on any single rendition of Atris. He had lost track of Ewan and his eyes could not translate the visual chaos. He closed them and focused his thoughts. Atris's visage appeared in his mind.

He slowly opened his eyes and remained fixated straight ahead, isolating an instance of Atris before making his way toward it. He concentrated on steadying his breathing. The shallowest draw felt as if he was inhaling the tempest from the river.

★★★★

Atris caught the waves of his brother closing on him as he vied for control. He staggered and brought his hand to his brow, suddenly recalling it all. He frantically filed recollections and revelations into loose categorizations, some rough order of events he could attempt to draw solutions from. He brought his gazes center to Arka and spoke in a tumult of echoing voices. "I remember."

13

Before I drive you in
before you wear me thin
before you forget yourself to know me instead,
take heed to all the chaos in your head.
Before the time to choose arrives
before we surrender our separate lives
before the higher caliber will arise,
remember you can't always trust your eyes.
Before these pages meet your stare
before I grow too indifferent to care
before you figure out what's there,
Run, run, run if you dare.

"Move!" Atris shouted as Ewan sprinted past him to begin the spiraling ascent up the stone tower. Arka had already reached the high tier and was readying the elevator. Fumbling with the heavy line, he shouted back down to his brothers, "We really gotta remember to make the last stretch of stairs next time. You know – the ones we keep talking about right around the time the scape goes to shit!"

"Noted!" Atris yelled, hot on Ewan's heels.

The quake was picking up, and the integration had to be fast approaching. They could still only speculate on the sequence of terminal events, the whys and wheres, never able to decipher a solid set of signals, triggers, or limitations. There wasn't a lot to draw from to deem safeguards or methods of evacuation when things started to fall apart.

When their surroundings began to deconstruct, creation became impossible. Atris would come to believe this was simply another facet of the body-mind safeguard mechanism, signaling the conscious mind it needed to return to reality immediately. The tremors were thus made the canary, and as long as the tower was close, the boys knew they could make it out in time.

Atris passed Ewan and jumped onto the platform while Arka grasped tightly on the line that stretched above some fifty feet to the top of the tower. What definition served as the moon was closing from directly overhead, its radiant halo enveloping their position as it descended upon the highpoint.

The wooden platform holding the three brothers had a circular cutaway in the center about a foot in diameter, with two lengths of rope passing through it from above. A pair of stabilizing poles ran through brackets in the corners closest to the tower column; with two support beams running at 45-degree angles beneath the platform to fasten to a vertical span up against the tower. As far as the boys had figured, the structure was sound. The design had been used before in the past, though they failed to remember exactly when they had constructed it or why they hadn't indeed fashioned stairs leading all the way up.

"Not much longer now," Ewan said, craning his neck to the sky and grabbing the tough line just above Arka's hands.

"Let's go!" Arka heaved the rope down and the lift jerked upward. Ewan followed suit as Atris hurled himself to the other side of the small platform via his own newfound grip at the rope's highest reachable point. The three of them toiled in flawless succession as the lift skipped up the line.

Ewan jumped up and drew the rope down once more, hitting the platform with a loud thud, followed by a sharp crack that menacingly vibrated the wood beneath their feet. Ewan looked Arka dead in the eyes. The stare was absolute and froze a second in time.

The platform gave out from under them and fell away, bouncing off the side of the tower below and disappearing into the black. Arka, Ewan, and Atris clung to the center line, as a large whizzing sound cut through the darkness above. The rope slackened and the boys fell ten feet before the line became taut again, nearly ripping their grips from their hands.

Arka looked up to see a steel ring wound through the failing winch serving as an anchor point as the single line they were holding began to fray. He watched it coming undone, looking down to see Ewan and Atris realize the same. The boys scrambled upward, racing the unwinding fibers to the top of the tower.

"We're not gonna make it!" Ewan shouted.

"Keep going!" Atris yelled from below him.

Arka savagely combated gravity in staggered volleys, convincing himself it couldn't be much further now. A loud snap split the air above, the unmistakable profile of splintering wood. Arka froze for a second and looked down at his friends. Atris met his eyes, then looked below.

"Don't!" Arka shouted wildly. Atris released his hold on the line, falling to the upper level of the spiral stairs. Arka cursed and strained feverishly, hoisting himself onto the winch beam and rolling onto the tower apex, whirling around to bring his hands to the edge. Ewan heaved himself up and crumpled behind his position, gasping for air.

"Atris!" Arka called down through the dust.

"You—" He was cut off by a loud whizzing sound followed by the clank of the support pulley as it furiously zipped the line through the winch. He could do nothing as the rogue pulley took the remaining rope with it and disappeared into the rising fog. The thunderous racket all around intensified. The descending light drew close.

Arka shouted into the miasma. "Don't get lost in here. We'll come back for you!"

The wind howled menacingly, fighting to divert his words from their intended receiver.

"Right! Time you got going then!" his friend's faint voice called from below.

Arka desperately searched for the right words to say in the seconds he had left. He analyzed their recent journey, the notions Atris was pulling out of the abyss, the girl, the hinted reluctance to leave, the look in his eyes when he let go. "Remember brother, Greer's dead! He can't come back!"

"I know he can't! But you better still come back for us!" Atris yelled.

Arka tensed, realizing that while Atris seemed to accept the matter of Greer, he still failed to comprehend his impending solitude. He remembered the argument that had occurred just moments before. Atris's hallucinations were getting the best of him. But again so soon? Was that why he gave up the rope so easily? Why he threw himself away? Arka knew who else Atris thought was being left behind with him.

"Atris!" His words echoed as the halo descended around and inward, "She doesn't exist! She never did!" His words were amplified, cast outward to resonate off the far mountains in the same instant the tower went from underneath him. A radiant light cut through the sky in a wave of brilliance.

★★★★

Arka fell to the floor in a tidal wave of recollection, thankful he was not met with the previous overpowering assault on the senses, observing Atris and Ewan as singularities once again.

"I felt like I was just there," Ewan whispered as he opened his eyes. Atris's face was in his hands.

"The relative significance of the fall must mirror another pivotal moment in time," Arka said.

"We thought we must come back to find a way to bring you home. Perhaps resolving to make it out of this twisted fantasy time and again, escaping before we would trade reality for the beautiful abandon of dreams.

Taking into account this risk, we had to return, unable to idly wonder what kind of ageless lunacy devoured you, unable to do nothing when we potentially had the power to pull you out."

Greer stepped in beside Arka, proverbial mace to his mind's eye. Arka was once again battered by further cherished memories, adventures that happened ages ago. He was shocked back to the task at hand when Ewan took hold of his arm.

Greer spoke, his words aptly fitting the drawn-out tone of a ghost. "We were forced to forge divisions. We became byproducts of notions you all pursued, concepts you were after through all your journeys."

Atris was looking down at the floor.

Greer shifted. "Concept-made manifestations originally conceived by all, the likes of which he found himself marooned here for entertaining too much in the first place, were developed and reinforced as his exile wore on."

Arka reached out to touch Greer, but his fingers fell through nothing, as fog breaking on a cold window pane. Greer didn't seem to notice and continued on.

"It was his fear. The fear of being trapped proved a force inconceivable to overcome. However, instead of materializing and playing out a hellish redundancy, he developed this notion of creation, far away from talk of physical vessels. Measures were taken to twist the nightmare back into dream."

★★★★

Atris slowly stood and steadied his footing, beating back crippling distress in hopes of dealing with the cancerous doubts subjugating his battered ego. What seemed like recollections from a hundred lives well lived were frantically browsed over, in wild attempts to organize what he might perceive as true within the tangled mess of illusions and memory.

Greer now stood with Atris to his left, Arka and Ewan to his right, between the council and the stairs. Atris ran his fingers over his head and sighed heavily. He spoke hesitantly, as if fighting the words from leaving his mouth. "There's no comprehending…"

Greer turned to face him. "We never consciously constructed anything in the scape. It was all already there. We amassed the grand library, all the while suppressing the fear-fueled notion that no one would come back. In turn, you moved to dismiss searching for a way out. You adapted, mapping out a stratagem for progress despite your entombment, when in fact you were only deceiving yourself. You couldn't erase and forget it altogether. You continued to hold onto hope, Atris." Greer began to fade into transparency. "Rather, you held onto her."

Arka reached out to spin Greer around but again his fingers passed through the air unhindered.

"Wait! Talk to me!" He took a swing at the image of his lost friend, his fist passing through what intangibility comprised the side of Greer's head.

Greer heeded the attempt and turned to face Arka.

"I am the past. Remember our times. Seek what will be yours, and forget what was mine."

"No, we're here for Atris. We can bring you back too!" Arka argued.

Greer was gone as quickly as he'd appeared. Atris regained the scope of his surroundings as Ewan seized hold of his arm. It seemed Ewan had irrevocably had it with the progression of events.

"What are you holding onto?" he shouted. "What does he mean – who are you holding onto?!"

Atris looked up as the heated voice of his brother, along with the steady rattle of the prevailing quake, faded to a low hum. Ewan's grip on his arm seemed to dissolve. Arka stood where Greer once had, angrily gazing off into the black.

A clap resembling that of a circuit breaker switch cut through the void and the ground instantly steadied, blinding whiteness claiming everything around. What was but a vast darkness, absent any visual features, gave way to a stretching field of grass the color of pale ivory. Atris's sight returned, drawing out varying hues of white.

14

We wander as before, across lands made new no more,
it's a serenade that resonates from the void between us as the years turn color
it's something I knew that grew from you
and our answers would be found if we never lose each other.
We say we were there to hear it
the closed be the ones who fear it
what grace is left to steer it
fires and facades, towers of time
our vessels search on as before.
And thus we are lost, for a hiatus we pray
which voices be the cost, our love be the way.

M enace no longer filled the air; chaos became tranquility. Atris was alone once again, sensing his priorities undergoing a monumental shift. He considered a new plan. *Plan.* The word never sat quite well with his lot. They had come to approach prospective intentions with prevailing caution as they aged. Apprehension concerning certainty was enforced by the general speculation that it was simply the safest manner to go about things. In truth, the formulating of solid, long-term plans was not in keeping with classic Runner tactics. Everything was usually impulse-driven, last-minute bouts of grandeur, more times than not yielding far greater excitement, with no risk of failure to meet set arrangements. They resolved to exchange plans for the simple drafting of ideas, a more malleable interpretation of the former, rough layouts of designs and dreams. Atris laughed to himself at this observation, in spite of its relative irony.

It was frivolous now, dogma followed a lifetime ago. Many interpreted these practices as the commonplace ideology of deliberately aiming low in order to never be let down. Atris thought the issue was a matter of increasing tenacity toward the fight, of being more aggressive to engage life with compounding fervor. The external antagonist changed as the years turned, but they could never escape themselves. And once they'd reached adulthood, it seemed like the fire had dwindled, freeing up time and energy for more stable causes, for logic and security. He figured they had just gotten tired at some point, from living too fast maybe. They grew to expect – and frequently receive – the worst case scenario, always preparing for a bad outcome, silencing optimistic hopes for sake of self-defense should wavering barricades collapse.

They were trapped already. They were trapped in time. In a certain duration of perceived reality, partaking of a general consciousness they wanted no part of. They were explorers born into a physically supposed world with no remaining frontier, growing up in an age where the proliferation of technology somehow led the majority of mankind astray, closing more minds than were opened.

They wanted to be part of the progressive frontline – not for any self-validation in light of individual gain, but simply because they wanted purpose. They wanted to be part of a selfless worldly consciousness, of humanity's will to achieve, of a general collective that fed off communal inspiration, measured in progression as a team, as a race.

Perspective, again, that's all it ever really was. Instead of the grandiose expectations they had for adulthood, they ended up instead with the opposite: a dulling down of the primal tendencies they capitalized on through adolescence – the very tendencies they embraced in order to truly feel alive, to feel a part of something grand, for better or worse. It was when these wildest of traits were called into play, when they were all-in, that true inspiration seemed to fill the air and lift their bleeding hearts skyward.

It was worlds easier for most to worry about the immediate scope of their own individual plans. Most members of society are consistently conditioned to care about where it is they are going or how long it will take to get there, weighing these factors against set priorities for worth against cost. People drift toward the path of least resistance, though it is not necessarily the most rewarding. There are endless things to miss if one spends their life traveling in straight lines all the time. As a species, we need to evolve beyond the easiest choices and comfortable surrenders. We need to believe in hope and wonder above all else.

The unknown is paramount, and people are losing faith. Everyone must admit the senses can easily be deceived. While some say seeing is believing; beliefs themselves aren't seen, they are felt. People are losing this faith because they are silencing their own curiosity and succumbing to fruitless distractions. The real art of keeping faith is finding a narrow passage through the bombardment of stimuli, through everyone else's noise and shallow goals.

Arka used to say, "The appropriate response to life's slings and arrows might seem to be making yourself steely hard, to don a coat of armor. That armor may soften the blows, but it weighs you down. It's not just what it keeps out that you should be concerned with, it's what it would keep locked in that worries me.

Instead, the answer is to make yourself soft and porous, remorseless. Soak up this life and whatever comes of it. The punishments, the rewards, take it all in. Hold your colors, don't forget who you are."

"Don't forget who you are," Atris said aloud. His thoughts were branching off in multiple spiraling directions, and he inhaled deep, searching for focus while lifting his head from thought to verify his solitude. Perhaps the others had made it out already. Maybe they hadn't even been there at all. The unwavering, concrete conviction he had wielded whilst explaining his agenda to Arka had given way to uncertainty. And here he remained.

Had he really died?

"No," he said calmly. "We'll figure this one out, even if there isn't much logic and reason to go on. We must progress, for without expansion into realms unknown will cold despair take over. Many people may as well be dead already, closed off from experience and growth. How can I be...?"

Atris's humility surfaced following the outlandish manner of his words and he barred himself from going into another bout of philosophical retrospection.

He closed his eyes. He remembered the fall. It ran vividly through his mind, clear and concise as a projection screen before him. The tower had come down all around, and the sky closed in, erasing the light of the moon, trading its luminescence for a mock impending dawn that would never arrive.

Atris saw himself wandering the halls of their library, paging through notebooks in the warm glow of the hanging candles. He remembered the cutting loneliness of that first stage, left only to their writings, ledgers and pictures of old. He recalled the way the land seemed to be dying. Each time he'd climb to the ruined tower, the mountainsides were less graced with life, their trees dwindling in number. What counted for sunlight occurred less and less, and steam from far-off fissures became evermore present, along with the quakes that wrought the massive cuts in the land. He believed he couldn't stop any of it because he had no one to compound his will. One mind wasn't strong enough.

He remembered his first trip below and how the only means of mental survival was to radically form things anew. He found Greer there, and together they talked of complex theories and uninterpretable possibilities. Atris sank for a moment, wondering where exactly on the timeline he had departed reality and what measures he had to take in order to hold onto some loose form of sanity.

All hopes of getting out of this place – of returning home, hopes of a bright true future, for better days, for measured time to exist again – he'd resigned to cast aside. Had he any choice but to make this work? What if the others never found a way back for him? What if this was his own manifest guilt taunting him?

Hope was a cherished thing indeed; he didn't take it for granted. Yet in here, alone, he suspected it would inevitably breed only doubt and despair, fuel for the rising fear that he constantly battled to keep at bay. Had he really forsaken all hope? All trace of salvation?

"Atris." The harmonious voice seemed to originate from everywhere.

He focused across the striking whiteness of the field once more, to the pale figure of a woman slowly approaching amidst a backdrop of pale-violet sky. She was adorned in a dress shining white as the ground she gracefully traversed, her footfalls barely disturbing the snow-white grass, evident of a manner in which she was weightless, almost floating. Her long hair fell about her shoulders in a red cascade. Atris felt relief in her presence. She grew closer to him, washing away all staining shred of worry with each stride. She outstretched her arms and brought her hands around his rough shoulders, leaning in to rest her head carefully against his chest.

Atris held her close and rifled through what sensibilities were left in his head, sifting through the widespread wreckage in an attempt to find the right explanation, the right words to say.

"I couldn't find you."

Aislin looked up into his shattered-glass irises and smiled in a form that weakened Atris's stance.

"You knew they would get here sooner or later, love." Her voice was soft on the faint breeze that passed.

"They might not have."

"You had faith. You believed. … Now you must go." Aislin's words ushered an unexpected urgency.

"Go? We're together again. Think what could be ahead of us." Atris tried to hang on.

Aislin released her embrace and shook her head slightly, her hair gently moving from side to side. "We know it won't be the truth. We've witnessed the old reality fall to ruin, you and I – a lesson in this test, a caution to destruction. Our brazen trail must continue on to parts unknown." She smiled at him with longing eyes.

Atris concentrated on his previous thoughts of hope for better days, of certainty, shifting perspective, expectations, and rekindling the wild rights of youth. The girl shining before him facilitated clarity.

"Aislin," he started in defeat. "You are all the grace that lies within a forlorn hope." His words came hard. "An angel whispering redemption."

She leaned in close, rising to press her pale cherry lips against his.

He recognized the feeling and, as she stepped back from him, Atris knew who stood before him was the very embodiment of brighter years. It all made sense now. She was an effigy within his own existence, a rendition of his aspirations and desire. As he existed in life, as matter perceiving time in a linear model, here he had constructed a body born of hope.

He realized now, looking into her tertiary eyes, that the fight he and his brothers felt in their youth was still breathing dormant. It was just a matter of will. All the previous methods of his youth, all the devices they used to chase happiness were all outdated.

They'd tried so hard to keep running, to keep the pace they set for themselves when they were young and could afford negligence. When in reality, in the world behind them now, life was indeed a fight. You can sit on the sidelines for as long as you want or you can play a few rounds before benching yourself for a while; but in order to succeed, in whatever varied adopted definition, one must always persist and progress. Seek to sharpen the mind and polish your wits, absorb life's lessons, tragic and true, beautiful and wretched the same. Evolve beyond your current perceptions.

Atris felt a resurgence in his heart, a lightness in his frame. His breath was coming easier. Inactive adherence to this twisted osmosis was what rendered his kind docile and cautious, as they cut risks for cost or concerns unworthy of the outcome. They had to resolve not to give in, to keep fighting.

Running was no longer the way.

Persistence is key; and above all else, hope.

He brought himself back to the field, realizing he had always loved the woman depicted before him, even though this might be the first time he had ever seen her. He took her hand in his.

Her soft voice graced his ears once more. "You must let me go, Atris. Live for the future, do not fight for the past. May hope not be a driving force locked away in shape."

Atris sighed as her face slipped into transparency. "Only in a dream could I ever define you."

She smiled back at him once more, "You're not dreaming. Don't lose our mind. There's still so much you've yet to find."

"Where?"

"We don't know, but that's the beauty of it." Aislin's hand slipped away with a chill, and she faded to nothingness.

Atris stood there for a moment, reeling through wild emotion.

"Let's move," he said to himself.

The ground beneath him rocked, its vibrations rising in severity at a steady pace. A stiff wind blew across the beautiful white field. Atris closed his eyes. The shaking increased.

15

Your doubts vein through a touch without the new
and waves take on ways from the radiating truth.
Blasting past the blindfolds of this race
we found them there
they told us they were shadows of our doomed grace
and we spoke and stared, stared, stared at the sky.
Holding on, we returned to those realms beyond reason
time and again we ran with our wind across fields
forsaking what was expected of us.
The sun shone down for our souls lit aflare
we found us there, we found us there.

Atris's vision widened to full, emerging from the darkest of tunnels. He saw Ewan and Arka shouting vehemently at each other, striving to beat out the loudening roar all around them.

"Brothers!" he cried. They both looked back at him in an even mixture of exasperation and relief. "Let's get out of here."

"Damn right!" Ewan shouted, whirling around and motioning for the stairs.

Arka crouched down to study Atris's eyes. "I thought we failed."

"No," Atris said calmly. "We are really here. We exist."

"And we've got to see how this one plays out," Arka said, grabbing Atris's shoulder.

"Look, that's great guys," Ewan muttered, "but let's get the hell out of here now! We are out of time, I'm not getting stuck."

Arka stepped toward him, "What did you say?"

"Look, we have to be out of time by now, that's why the quake is getting worse, right?" Ewan replied. "Signals to leave?"

"We're out of time," Arka whispered. He glanced at Atris. "But then how are we–?"

"The vortex." Atris rose to his feet.

"The quantum spike. It affected our original timeline in the manner of a vortex, or a whirlpool profile, distorting multiple instances into simultaneous variations, spiraling vertically off our linear model."

"So? What's that mean for us?" Ewan pried. "You forget the fall again already? What about the other times we've been here?"

Atris exhaled slowly, assessing the components of his explanation. "Well. … They could have all just happened."

Ewan's blank stare conveyed his loss for words.

Arka shifted under the weight of the revelation. "I thought we'd been here many times before. I thought we created all this over the years – the library, the land, the structures. When in fact, they're all separate occurrences, translations or memories within our minds. When we first came here together, when Atris fell, and how we are here now – they're all happening together somehow."

Ewan went pale. "Sure guys, but we're still going home, right?"

"I don't know where we are going," Atris said, finally making his way for the stairs.

Ewan raced to catch up. "All this time, and we might get up there to have what happen? Nothing?"

"We go north," Atris calmly replied.

"The ocean?!" Ewan turned back to Arka, who only shrugged and motioned for him to follow Atris.

"No. We're not following the old definition of north, not heading toward a magnetic polar cap that no longer exists for us." Atris paused. "This translation will be our own."

"Forgive me for not sharing in your excitement," Ewan rattled. "If what Arka here says is true, I'm following a dead man through bent time to an unknown end! ... I want to go home. The playoffs are next month, I think, the concert a couple weeks after that. And what if they don't have beer where we're going? I'm just going to miss all the shit I like because you triggered some rift? I didn't sign up for this."

"We didn't consciously sign up for anything, man," Arka replied. "Though perhaps it's what we've been waiting for all these years. We were searching for the unknown, and now here we are, on the precipice of something incredible and beyond the scope of our comprehension. A damn-all journey into mystery."

"There are parts of us that are moving to another level," Atris added. "I'd say there might be others that stay behind. Or perhaps we may leave renditions in this place should we wake up and this turns out to be a lucid nightmare. Consciousness, just like time, is relative."

Ewan wrestled with the notion, "Like maybe how Mary was part of—"

Arka cut him off. "None of us are sure what will happen or where we are going, but the theory is you won't miss your life happen."

Ewan sighed. "I guess we don't have a choice anyway."

"Let's move," Atris decreed.

They nodded and leapt up the glass stairs to the lower hall of the archives, sprinting up the marble staircase toward the main chamber. The deafening quake was shaking the books from their shelves as a lantern came detached from the wall and shattered against the hard marble. The building felt as if it might come down at any minute. Then the massive skylight gave way and a showering cascade of glass bore down upon them.

Ewan looked up at the coming death with a pitiful frown. Arka didn't break stride, sacking him into one of the bookshelves. Atris dove into the preceding shelf, tipping its weight over on top of his comrades and shimmying in beside them a mere second before the rain of glass crashed throughout the great hall.

"Dammit. How can things get any worse?" Atris sighed from behind his sleeve as thousands of glass shards rang about the marble floor.

"Don't ask that!" Ewan demanded. The echoes of shattered glass ceased and the three strained under the weight of the shelf to lift it vertical once more. Arka brushed himself off and studied the gaping hole in the roof.

"Lightning strike?" Atris posed. "Or maybe the roof buckling?"

"Nope." Arka quivered. From the edges of the newborn entryway overhead, came a multitude of blackened arms groping about the jagged glass. The eerie appendages were followed by black figures clinging to the ceiling, crawling their way out to the walls.

"Spiders?! Are you serious?" Ewan asked in disbelief.

"Uh. ... Run!" Atris dashed off across the giant embossed star. Arka and Ewan followed without hesitation. The figures didn't make a sound, but it was evident they intended the boys prey. The three Runners soared from open space into the rows of shelves, glass crunching beneath their feet. Loud thuds sounded about the walls as puffs of ash shot up to choke the remaining candlelight.

Soon the boys were running through shadow, the marble floor reflecting what traces of light it could through the gaping ceiling.

"Where are we going?" Ewan shouted.

"The back stairs," Atris yelled from point.

They were about to bound up the last marble staircase and into the small vestibule when their path was barred. Several dark figures blocked the hall's exit. The boys ducked right and into the grid of bookshelves.

"The hell are those things!?" Ewan made his shout a whisper. They fought to suppress their collective breathing as the sound of heavy footsteps fanned out between the adjacent shelves. The boys huddled there, knowing it was not the time for words. One of the creatures stepped around the shelf, not five feet away. Atris looked over to Arka, who nodded. They both glanced at Ewan.

Teeth clenched, muscles primed, adrenaline surging, the boys launched up and into the cover of their shelf. The wood groaned, and a black hand appeared overtop just before the bookcase toppled over, sending ash billowing out from underneath. The boys jumped atop the shelf as the desired domino effect ensued.

They sprang about the falling shelves, riding the wave, eluding ghastly outstretched reaches.

Overtaking the last set of marble stairs, they ran through the vestibule and made for the tunnel. Atris dashed hard, right up narrow spiraling steps, Arka on his heels. Ewan followed, snapping a nearby lantern from its mount with a loud creak. He whirled it around and sent it sailing into the torso of one of their assailants, igniting it immediately.

"Hah!"

Arka grabbed him by the arm and pulled him to the stone steps. Blazes flared up from the vestibule. The antagonists' positions quickly became indisputable. Half a dozen figures set ablaze marched toward them.

"Well that sucked." Ewan turned and fled with Arka, bound for the roof.

★★★★

"Oi! Ewan!" Brac shouted, rounding the ramp as it became level.

An aged Ewan turned suddenly, his look of surprise shifting to confusion. "The hell are you doing here man? Whatever – give me a hand!" He threw a length of rope to Brac.

"Aren't we supposed to be fixing some sort of elevator?" Brac asked.

"No time. Most of the wood's splintered to shit. Won't hold." Ewan hurled one end of his own rope aloft. "I thought there was some point at which we could create something, make this all work, but I haven't the slightest." The end of the rope fell a few feet from them, having overtaken something above. Brac looked up to see a web of thick branches extending from the tower's pinnacle, rich with radiant leaves that threw out whites and purples taken from the shimmering moonlight.

"Toss that last one over," Ewan ordered. "I gotta tie this down." He rounded the bend, coming upon a massive, gnarled tree root that seemed to protrude straight from the tower column.

Atris, Arka, and Ewan came hurdling out of the attic, stopping for nothing on their way over to the tower's base. The sky was littered with storm clouds and forked lightning, the landscape in all directions choking under a blanketing layer of steam and fog. Only the scattered peaks of tall, trembling mountains rose out of the gray.

Atris slowed to admire the view. "Magnificent, isn't it?"

"Keep moving!" Arka snapped. They raced upward until the ramp leveled out flat, some seventy feet above the archives' roof.

"About damn time!" Brac shouted.

"Ewan!" Atris shouted back down the ending spiral stair. "Cover your eyes!"

"Already got him blindfolded," Arka said, leading young Ewan up the last part of the incline.

"Right," Atris said. They were all together once more, at the final point of flight. "We've made it."

Arka laughed. "Yeah, but—"

"We're not out yet!" Ewan's aged variant sneered. "I couldn't fix the lift for nothin'. It took you guys forever to get here. I'm so done with this shit. You know how hard it is—"

"Hold on!" Arka interrupted. "Are you telling me we're done? Thirty feet from the finish line?"

"No!" Ewan retorted. His voice paired with an explosion in the distance as another mountain vomited a dark pillar of ash and fire into the sky. "There was plenty of rope left from the wreckage."

Arka and Atris looked beyond Ewan to Brac, who was scaling one of the three ropes that hung from branches overhead. The other ends stretched down and were affixed to knotted roots inhabiting the upper rotunda around the bend from where they stood.

"It's the strangest thing," the elder Ewan continued. "Must've completely forgotten about this tree – just like everything else I guess, hope you guys are in for a good climb."

"That's 'cause it wasn't there other times," Atris said.

"How can it even survive up here?" Arka wondered. "Everything else is dying." He grabbed the third line and started his own ascent.

"This is something else," Atris replied. "Growing of something else." He swore he could hear the playful laughter of a girl ride by on the wind as he led young Ewan over to the lines and placed one in his hand.

"Come on!" Brac called down at them. Atris could barely make him out against the rays of light cutting through the rustling leaves.

"Wait a minute!" Ewan turned away from the ropes. "Where–"

A loud roar resounded throughout the sky as another mountain on the horizon split straight down its center.

"Hurry up!" Arka shouted from above, Brac and young Ewan at his sides. Atris ran for the ropes, Ewan shouted something again from behind him, something indiscernible.

The two remaining travelers toiled feverishly; hand over hand, two or three stories up what they hoped would be the last stretch of their mad journey. Atris couldn't look directly up. The moon was virtually upon them, in all its blinding glory. Trails of light were coming from all around, dancing downward gracefully; a lunar rain in a wondrous shimmering cavalcade. Atris's hands continued skyward until they found the rope's anchor point as it overtook the branch. He felt his way to the right and reached out for aid, Brac's hand catching his firmly. He leapt over and onto the towering zenith.

"We made it!" Arka shouted at the sky, barely heard amidst the thunderous rumble.

Atris stood and saw his friends about him, in the midst of dancing ribbons of light extending down and inward from the collapsing halo. He glanced over the edge to the building below. Fire had spread to a good portion of the upper level and smoke vented out the compromised roof. He subdued mounting sorrow for the amassed library, as if watching ancient Alexandria burn.

He sighed and embraced the white light; it was all they were now. He heard faint voices from close by, barely discernable amidst the surging gust stripping the giant oak of its leaves in a rising whirlwind. At first it sounded as if it was some sort of argument, but he wrote it off as Ewan's boasting or Brac's cheering.

There was a deafening crack from below. Everyone jumped onto the low branches. The tower was about to give way beneath their feet.

It was all right though. Gravity was gone. Atris felt like floating.

"We thought he was with you!"

16

This single theory cultivates comfort in the timing of woes
though balanced and brandished is polished paranoia kept in waked old
living in the gray verse living the way your breath wants to go.
Don't resign. Life is music, though you must keep time.
It's a simple assessment really, whatever way the wind went naturally
the worth of the use, the sell for the fall
factors and virtues, lenience recall
fortify and fight on, on to the next act.
It's the people, not the days, that keep you coming back
decades defined what came to be families
now in the light of the ages, it's our turn to fashion someone else's pages.

A tris opened his eyes and took a deep breath, moving next to sit up
from the forest floor.

"Sure is a nice night," Ewan said, seated a few feet to his left. He
hunched forward and threw a small stick into the low fire.

"Yeah, check out that moon," Arka said, emerging from the darkness and adjusting his belt before sitting down himself.

The three gazed up through the opening in the treetops wrought of their small clearing, with the moon just overhead. A gigantic, faint ring of light circled it some three feet as the naked eye could perceive. Atris had seen it before, but he couldn't remember when.

He lowered his vision and sighed in contentment, gazing across the dancing flames.

Aislin was beautiful sitting there, the orange shimmers playing off her fair complexion. She laughed gently as she looked up from the pages of the book and smiled at him.

"Run."

"No," Atris whispered. The lights hit the trees from far off.

"Bail!" Ewan shouted.

Atris didn't comply. Instead, he slowly stood up with his sights set on Aislin. She smiled again and rose to meet him.

"No," he repeated lowly. He turned to see Ewan and Arka were gone, moving still to observe the lights getting closer. He sighed heavily and glanced over his shoulder to see Aislin had vanished as well.

"No!" he cried out to the sky. He ran full sprint through the woods, dodging branches, roots, and bitter doubt. "Dying to know, just where we'll go now," he muttered under his breath. He headed directly for the lights.

The haloed moon granted enough light to discern immediate depth and maintain his flight in the cold dark. Minutes passed as he grew closer to his target. He broke through the forest to come upon the light in a cleared path. It disappeared and gave way to total darkness, the absolute static black left in the wake of brightness, his eyes attempting to account for its absence the following instant after it was seemingly all there was. He paused to catch his breath and stared at the sky.

"What am I doing here?" He took a few steps down the path. "What went wrong?"

The next second saw the reappearance of the lights far off to the right of the path, followed by a single beam suddenly upon him. No, this was smaller. ... This was someone.

Atris crossed his arms and grit his teeth as he realized who had found him.

"Look, we've got to move," he hesitantly told the figure with the headlamp. "There is no time left." He pointed off in the direction of the lights before charging toward them once more.

There had to be a way to fix this. The end of their time in the scape had dumped him right back at the beginning, but why? Were the lights merely transports to places he'd already been? He resolved to remain confident as he closed in on them once more, running relentlessly and catching a low branch against his cheek. The sharp pain filled his mind with his friend's image. *That's it. ... Nico. You didn't stick to the plan, and now look at you.*

He clenched his jaw and charged hard, flying over the last wooded stretch and vaulting upon the lights for another attempt. Gravity paused, his feet didn't hit the ground, and he was seized by a fierce sensation pulling him forward through blinding white.

★★★★

Arka opened his eyes as he landed softly on loose dirt. Recovering, he gazed around the field to find silhouetted figures far off. He had been overcome with a mix of uneasy excitement and relief as the torrent tore the leaves from the oak. Realizing he had been here before, these feelings quickly morphed into fledgling terror. He wasn't sure what would happen, though he had found comfort in everyone making it there together – that is until Ewan shouted Nico's name as the light took them.

Arka ran up on the circle of silhouettes to find they were not of his friends. Point of fact, he couldn't tell who they were at all. He could only discern three humanoid statures upon focusing his vision, each blurred illuminant of a different color. The prismatic aura of this place shot different shades everywhere. There was nothing else remarkable beyond the vivid circle. If this was to be his limbo, he thought, at least it was appealing to the eyes.

"Nico!" he called out to the sky.

★★★★

Nico staggered backward across fallen books and allowed his back to thud against the wall. He had searched most of the building for Aislin, only the upper level still remained when the skylight came down. The dark figures were everywhere now and he opted to hide for rest. He didn't know how much fight was left in him, a suspicion breeding irritation in the exhaustion, even if the dream had decisively shifted into a nightmare. The upper hall had caught fire and he couldn't find anyone.

He hoped there was still time to escape, but was there even a point? Slumping low onto the cold floor, he wondered if this was the type of situation where he must give in to get out. He closed his eyes. There was Aislin. She smiled through space, heeding Nico's sight and drawing closer to him.

"Run," she said softly.

Nico opened his eyes to see a bookshelf topple over the banister above. He sprang forward and out from under the trajectory of the flaming mass just before it splintered on the hard marble.

"No," Nico said to himself. "No point in staying still. Better keep moving." He had to keep fighting for control. He had never given in, and he wasn't about to start now.

The high fire was picking up momentum, leaving the lower hall the only possible way out. He bounded for the lower level, where Arka had collapsed. It was his only shot left.

The ash-men picked up on his movement and took chase, leaping from the higher levels and across the main hall. Nico nearly fell down the last few steps, but regained his footing and ran over to the glass staircase. The darkness below was daunting. It couldn't really be where Atris had gone to look for Greer, could it? The persistent rumbling vibrated a metal lantern that had been discarded nearby. Nico ran to the walls, reaching up to tear one of the last remaining lanterns from its mount with an unnerving screech. He turned to head to the glass stairs, but was cut off by five ashen figures, a dozen more descending from the main hall behind them.

Nico sighed heavy as they moved to surround him. He brandished the lantern, the wax within smote the flame as it soared into the head of an attacker, resulting in a burst of black. Nico backed up against the wall and squared off.

"If this is it," he said to himself. "Maybe I'll come back for every last one of you." He charged in hard, landing a strong uppercut to one and a following elbow strike to the next. Flailing wildly, he was soon lost in a cloud of ash. It was impossible to see but a couple feet ahead as his attackers came from all directions.

White light instantly penetrated everything around him, driving the choking veil hard to the walls. Nico staggered back and fell against the wall himself, observing a fair portion of the small army unfortunately still on their feet. The vanguard, however, had been seized by concentrated light as they violently jolted in electrifying spasms, spitting out trails of white, orange, purples, and blues to the ceiling. The radiance grew to blinding caliber, accompanied with a sharp ringing.

"What the shit?!" Ewan shouted through the delirium.

The light faded to reveal Ewan, Brac, Arka, and Atris standing between Nico and the regrouping line of ash-men occupying the floor above.

"Never thought it'd be so good to see you guys," Nico said as he held his arm.

"How … are we?" Arka trailed off.

Atris walked over to Nico. "You know it's probably dangerous to wander this place alone."

Ewan turned and rushed to Nico's aid. "Shit, we're here for you, aren't we? Now we gotta fight our way to the top again?" He helped Nico to his feet. The ash-men were accumulating on the main level but strangely didn't advance to the lower hall.

"How is it?" Arka questioned again. "Did we not make it?"

"No," Atris said abruptly. "We had to have made it."

"How do you know?" Ewan asked indignantly.

Atris looked over to Nico, "Because we are still here."

Ewan was unconvinced. "We're trying to leave! Why are we still in this place? Why didn't the tower tree thing work? It doesn't make any sense!"

"It doesn't have to make sense," Atris declared. "The criteria a particular notion must meet in order to 'make sense' must change as we move forward. We have to learn to think differently, counter-intuitively even."

"What?!" Ewan threw his hands in the air. "Enough with the cryptic shit!"

Arka nodded. "Well, think about the phrase. It labels the matter in question depending on what seems real or reasonable to our sensory perceptions, thus making sense."

Brac chuckled. "Wow. We're all going mad."

"No brother," Atris reassured. "It's just beyond our understanding. Look!" He pointed at the shattered skylight. The tower still stood firm above.

"Well that doesn't help us down here," Ewan said.

"Don't you see, man?" Atris stepped into the middle of the room. "We are passing through channels we cannot comprehend yet, traveling via some intangible method – some unseen catalyst."

"Seems likely," Brac conceded. "Though we don't have any control over where we end up next."

Arka sighed. "Yeah, I don't want to be thrown into a ditch again or another lost funeral memory. How do we get out of here for real?"

Nico cleared his throat. "Yeah, this is a cute conversation guys, but we really don't want those things to come back."

"The hell are they anyway?" Ewan kicked an ash-strewn skeletal structure sprawled on the ground.

Atris walked over to it. "They're failed connections. ... Negativity translated into physical forms."

"Still, how do we escape? We fight our way back up?" Arka posed.

"And what if we fail again?" Ewan added. "Are we stuck in some sick loop?"

"We can't fail," Atris said.

Nico eyed him. "Why not?"

"Because we made it already. Because we must somehow be occurring in multiple places. Because time doesn't matter, time isn't matter, and we can find another way."

"If at first you don't succeed deal?" Brac gibed.

"No," Atris said.

Ewan looked around the structure, "This buildings gotta be ready to go any second."

"Why do you think we call 'em seconds?" Arka inquired.

Ewan shook his head. "Shit."

"There's just," Atris said thoughtfully. "–there's something we haven't figured out, something we missed."

"Like what?" Nico asked.

Atris looked up. "I'm not sure. We have everyone now."

Arka leaned against a nearby reading table, steadying it against the vibrating floor. "Not everyone." They all followed Arka's gaze to the tunnel opening set in the eastern wall of the room.

Ewan sighed heavily. "Wait a minute, hold on. You said we're occurring multiple places, so that means we are on the tower right now as well?

Atris walked over to Arka. "It's possible."

"Wasn't the whole point to make it to the top before the moon fell, or the lights got there or what?" Ewan asked.

"It was," Brac affirmed. "It's like he said. We missed something."

"Atris," Arka started. "...You remember Juli?"

The lights went out, and the rumbling floor slowed to a churning sensation. Atris felt the lull of automation, followed by the unmistakable rhythmic clicking of train tracks, coupled with his steady breathing. It was now all he heard.

"Guys?"

No answer.

The platform banked right, and Atris stabilized himself against a nearby partition. The ground lurched upward, and dim light infiltrated the windows to reveal a train car, with the buildings outside smearing together in trace luminescence. Atris looked to the rear of the compartment to find a girl shadowed there, longingly gazing out the side window. He suppressed the urge to rush over to her, adjusting for composure as he carefully made his way down the car.

The train banked left and light penetrated the dark corner, presenting an empty seat. Atris stopped short and looked back to the front. The new shadows of the right side sure enough enveloped a female figure. A portion of her ashen-blonde hair was all that stretched out into the light. He caught a glimpse of her eyes before another turn bent the rays of light to replace her.

Atris saw nothing but spoke confidently. "Juli."

"...You came back."

"Where are you? How are you in all of this?" he asked.

"Lost. Lost for a long time, on an endless track." Her voice sang from all around him. "I don't recall just how I–"

"Don't worry about it. I'm here now, somehow." Atris stepped forward, scanning the car but still seeing no one.

"You've been here before, but nothing is real anymore." The train gradually disappeared below ground, the surface rescinding its light. "Alone in the end." Her words echoed quietly in the dark.

"I'm still here, Juli."

"Here in this purgatory?"

Atris exhaled. "Let's move on."

"How? … Where?" Juli asked. "We can't go back."

"We're not going back," Atris said. "We have to be wayward and remorseless, open to endless possibility from here on out."

"The way the wind flies," Juli whispered.

Atris turned to see her seated behind him.

He maintained some distance as he continued. "We have to shed all desire to return to what we knew, have to discard whatever pieces we are holding onto."

"The pieces are all I have left," Juli interjected in distaste.

"I know," Atris acknowledged. "For as long as I can remember, I've been holding onto fragments of the past. I was ever-recording moments in time, fashioning shadows, whispers, and echoes of what we perceived throughout our lives. There were marked moments where my heart soared. I felt weightless, unbound, and absolutely free. And in truth, I didn't feel real; I felt better. I consistently fought to document some shred of that sensation."

Juli looked at him listlessly, and he sighed in turn.

"Originally, I thought that was the end goal through this whole mad journey – to get back home before something unthinkable happens. But the unfathomable has been happening all around us. Our minds have been trying to decipher what segments they can, translating energy or waves or some other force into the matter we lived and learned with."

"But we aren't alive, are we? We can't go home," Juli shyly attested.

"We conceive a new home, a new realization," Atris proposed. "A new state of mind."

"And when we are no longer satisfied with our homes, we adapt, we find new ones."

The motion had stopped and Atris became aware of stationary ground. Embers appeared and reflected off Juli's face as she sat beside him.

He extended his arm to her.

"Whatever is next, we can go together, Juli. … Sometimes all we need is a friend to pull us out of the dark."

Juli despondently reached for his hand. He wrapped his fingers tightly around her wrist, and her body tensed solid. The ground fell away, taking the coal bed with it. Atris somehow remained affixed to a horizontal stage and unfalteringly maintained his hold.

★★★★

Juli saw steam rise up amidst an orange glow, and a length of rope fall from the left of Atris's position. He was gone, though something still clung tightly to her as she swayed in suspension.

The loud hiss of a geyser shot up mere feet away. She watched it recede as the echoes of a loud rumble encased her. Looking up again, she could see streaks of fire in a void high above, emanating from a billowing cloud of ash. She blinked and was met with the vague blur of a marble hall, bookshelves leaning against banisters as the rumbling persisted.

Still, whatever force was Atris's hand just seconds ago held true. What perceptions she made out against the trauma ran together, transforming in spinning motion and launching upward in an iridescent spiral. The shaking amplified, and Juli cried amidst the overwhelming brightness that followed.

17

The ones that came before us left their marks on the paths we came to call our own.

Ancient lost highways, flash forests drowning out their footprints as our whole generation continues to search for the forgotten home.

We couldn't read the schedule; it simply would not come into focus. The beggar told us of a compass of light, though clearly it had failed him as he lost his own way. I remember picking up speed, racing the storm for shelter; destination of the coast, the shore was all we'd need. We were fine with losing sense of self in gain for one another. But in these new days, how do we recover? We scaled mountains and ascended towers serving sentinels ever watchful for hell. Making these places our own in ways no words could sell.

There were times when all was right and the stars were ours. There were times to run, to stand and fight, to claim our battle scars in light of reckless, twisted glory. And our stories would echo down to those that aimed to follow us in turn. A rare breed of wonder forged from within. Nourished, reinforced through trials beside the truest of kin.

And whatever we meant to ranks not our own – passing relations, merchants, wavering nomads under the same sun – our band always knew just who to rely on *at the end of the day, when menace blocked our way, when the fabric of reality would start to come undone.*

For we are the Runners, we are rampant, we are one. We've walked with giants; we've split the earth, expelled magic into the sky. We've loved, we've hated through our tales of wonder, under the skies our lost god created. We've lived as kings; we've toiled in the slums. We've split the seams of the dream of a life they kept telling us to chase. The means may be hidden but the motive's still right in our face.

We see this one through together, as we always have. These dark days of uncertainty will be laid to rest. The bright rays of eternity wait as our hearts eagerly pulse in our chests. We are enlightened, we are one. We are the misplaced children of the sun. We'll never lie down; we'll always have the Run.

A tris closed his notebook and sheathed his pen at his side. Arka walked up behind him, soft soil packing beneath his feet. "You still trying to document it?"

"Old habits die hard," Atris admitted as he stood up, leaving his book where it lie. Colors shot all through the air and shimmering pillars of iridescence lulled in suspension a few feet behind them.

Juli approached with a smile. "Ready?"

"It seems we are," Atris affirmed, making his way to join the others by the radiant pillars.

"What comes next you think?" Brac asked.

"There's no way to know for sure, though we will journey forward, ever fighting, ever progressing. ... We will explore."

A Note to Readers

I wanted to take a moment to extend my sincere gratitude for investing your time in my book. If you are so inclined, please leave a review on Amazon or goodreads.com. As this is my first published work, I'd greatly appreciate any feedback. I am currently working on another novel as well as a collection of short stories. Feel free to contact me on Google+ or by email at douglasrblack04@gmail.com. Thanks again, and I hope you enjoyed the journey.

- Douglas R. Black

About the Author

Douglas Black resides in Asheville, NC. An all-around fan of exploration and human determination, he believes everyone possesses an extraordinary story within. He channels his filtered years here to submit his debut novel.